The WONDER OF YOU

USA TODAY Bestselling Author

CLAIRE MARTI

THE WONDER OF YOU

PACIFIC VISTA RANCH, BOOK 5

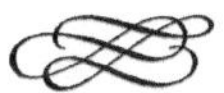

CLAIRE MARTI

THE WONDER OF YOU

Pacific Vista Ranch, Book Five

Copyright © 2021 by Claire Marti

ISBN: eBook: 978-1-7333046-8-9

ISBN: Paperback: 978-1-7333046-9-6

Published By: Claire Marti

Editor: Lindsey Faber

Proofreader: RickRack Books

Cover Design: Sarah Paige -The Book Cover Boutique

Discreet Cover: Vanilla Lily Designs

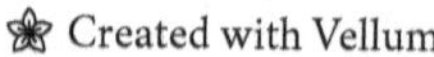 Created with Vellum

*For the forever friends who know you for who you are
and love you anyway.*

CHAPTER 1

Grant Michaels tapped his glass against the one held by Toby, one of his two childhood best friends. He tossed back the tequila and bit into a generous slice of lime, which failed to cut the acrid taste. Instead of the advertised smooth liquid fire, the alcohol seared his throat like burning lava. He disguised his choking with a cough.

Grant wiped his eyes, which much to his humiliation, were leaking like he'd been chopping onions. "Hey, don't judge. I haven't taken a shot in probably ten years."

Toby chuckled, set his glass down, and slapped his back. "So, you didn't drink much tequila in Australia then?"

"Beer. Tooheys New. Wine. And no shots." Grant grimaced and dipped a warm tortilla chip into the best guacamole in North County San Diego. The explosion of creamy dip and the perfect amount of spice hadn't changed in the last five years. He stretched his legs out, crossing his ankles under the scarred wood table at Fidel's, one of their old haunts from high school.

Stepping through the landmark restaurant's wide entrance tonight was like traveling back in time. The same mariachi music blasted through the speakers, the same scents of chilies and peppers and cilantro, the same high-back wooden booths. Flashbacks to simpler days, where he, Toby, and Olivia had immediately become inseparable. They'd done everything together, from surfing and snowboarding to studying. And when they'd each traversed through family tragedy and trauma, their unconditional bond was cemented further.

Hell, they'd even gotten matching tattoos after Olivia decided they were the Three Musketeers. A cool design with symbols from the book: a sword, a diamond, and a fleur-de-lis. They remained the two people he could count on through thick and thin.

Toby flashed a grin. "That's fair. But we had to do one for old times' sake. Now you can drink beer. I bet Livvie will down hers like a champ."

Grant nodded. "Right? Damn, it's been years since I've seen her. FaceTime and emails just aren't the same. How's she doing?"

"Definitely better now she has her own place. But ask her yourself when she gets here." Toby's bushy red eyebrows drew together. "How's it being back? I mean, how are you really?"

Returning to San Diego after his marriage had imploded had been humbling, but being close to family and now his best friends, who weren't constantly judging him, was worth it. One of the main reasons he'd left the international tour circuit was to see if he could be happy settling down in one place. His ex-wife—well, almost officially his ex-wife—Callie made it crystal fucking clear she thought he couldn't.

But no need to brood. Not tonight. "I'm okay. Living in one of the guesthouses on the ranch, and it's good to be close to my mom and Chris and my sisters." His mom had gotten remarried to Chris McNeill, a few years after they'd lost his dad. Chris owned Pacific Vista Ranch, a two-hundred-plus acre horse breeding ranch in Rancho Santa Fe.

"Your mom is the best. Does she miss me? Don't you think you should ask Angela to make those incredible tamales and invite your best buddy over?" Toby grinned and shoveled a handful of chips into his mouth.

"The more the merrier with her. I'm up at the main house for dinner with everybody more than I expected. She'd love to see you––everybody would." Grant sipped his beer, which soothed the raw inferno that was now his throat.

When Toby waved one lanky arm toward the hostess stand, Grant looked up. He straightened in the hard wooden booth when he caught sight of a stunning brunette. *Whoa.*

Like Olivia, the woman sauntering toward the table was petite with a tumble of long dark hair. Sure, like Olivia, she wore jeans and a black leather motorcycle jacket.

But where his best friend usually wore casual Chucks, this goddess strolled toward them wearing knee-high spike-heeled boots, her legs long and dangerous. Definitely not simply lean and athletic, which was his customary impression of his quirky librarian friend.

Like one of the guys.

Okay, like one of the guys––most of the time.

Even though she was his best friend, one of the guys, objectively he recognized she was pretty, with her enormous cornflower-blue eyes and delicate triangular face. But nothing about Olivia was delicate––she was tough, a warrior, and that was one of the many reasons the three of them had bonded.

This woman looked sexy and hot and edible. He shifted uncomfortably in his seat. Maybe that tequila shot had fried some brain cells, because obviously he'd lost his goddamn mind. Edible? Olivia? Livvie? He gripped his beer bottle and ground his back molars––*pull it together, dude.*

The restaurant might be exactly the same, but Olivia Hanlon undeniably was not.

She spotted him and flashed a broad grin. She hurried the last few steps to the booth, her arms thrown wide. "Grant." Joy filled her smooth voice.

He rose, grabbed her in a bear hug and swung her around. She burrowed against him, turning to press one cheek against his chest. Even with her high-heeled boots, her head only reached his chin. The scent of fresh peaches and honey enveloped him and he caught himself before he pressed his lips into her thick, silky mane.

What was wrong with him tonight?

She squeezed him tighter, her slender arms deceptively powerful. Back in the day, she'd beat both him and Toby in arm wrestling matches. Even though she was probably five feet two, one-hundred-ten pounds soaking wet. Hell, she could probably still take them both--maybe her day job consisted of hauling stacks of books instead of archiving them. She was wiry and as strong as Toby, who had been a pro snowboarder. She shifted back, gripped Grant's biceps, and gazed into his eyes.

"How are you? I can't believe we've let so much time go by. I've missed you so much." Her eyes gleamed in the dim light, her expression soft.

Had she always been this smoking hot? Usually when they'd video chat, she didn't wear makeup. Tonight, her mouth was fire-engine red, which was disconcerting. It high-lighted her full lower lip and perfect white teeth--honed from three years of braces in high school. Something about her just seemed different.

"Hello? Earth to Grant." She dropped her gaze to the table, spotting the two empty shot glasses, and turned to Toby who was still seated. "Did he forget how to speak or did you guys drink all the tequila without me?"

She released him, peeled off her jacket to reveal a snug V-neck black sweater, and slid into the booth. Without flinching, she tossed back her shot.

Grant found his voice again and sat down. "Sorry. One shot was enough for me. It's been too damn long, Livvie." His hand lifted to pat her shoulder, but he thought better of touching her right now when his body seemed to have forgotten she was his friend. Not some stunning stranger.

"I'm so glad you're home and I'm so sorry it's taken so long for us all to get together, especially since you've been back for months." She beamed at them both before looking around the bar. "Do we have a waitress or…"

Toby's phone buzzed. "Let me grab this call and I'll order another round while I'm up. Drink the rest of mine, but don't eat all the chips." He scooted his Mexican ale across the table for Olivia and strode off toward the restaurant entrance.

Grant pushed away his wayward thoughts and sipped his beer. He would ignore Livvie's appearance and treat her as he always had—like his best friend. "So what's with the red lipstick?" Damn it, what was wrong with him tonight?

Livvie's eyes widened. "Seriously? I've seen you practically every week on FaceTime for the last five years."

Grant ran his tongue around his teeth. "Sorry. You just look…different."

"Umm…would you care to rephrase?" She drummed her slender fingers on the table.

"You look beautiful. And sorry, I've been spending more time with horses than people these days." He scrubbed his hand along his jaw and realized he'd forgotten to shave. Again.

She tilted her head to one side and gave him a considering glance. "I'll forgive you this time because I'm just so happy we're all together. And don't take this the wrong way, but you look kind of rough. You okay?"

He shrugged and took another sip of beer. Hell, he hadn't figured out how he truly was.

"Getting there. I haven't been sleeping great. I'm still helping Sam on the ranch and starting to put out some feelers."

She shifted closer and another hint of juicy peach reached him. "But you're really home for good now? You didn't change your mind about returning to the pro tours?"

"I don't know. I've been taking a break from all of it. Maybe I'm getting old, but I'd like to be in one place more. Travel less. It's just tough with what I do––they won't have the X-Games or world-class tournaments at the ranch." And he was too damn old to bunk on the floor and party like he used to.

Her dark brows drew together. "Right. Well, you could focus more on surf photography, right? There are all kinds of local competitions and Hawaii isn't too far away."

"Maybe. I'm just wiped out. Travel to and from Australia was a major production. The time change, the distance, all of it. It burned me out and sure as hell didn't help my marriage."

She leaned forward and covered his hand with her slim one. "I'm so sorry it didn't work out with you and Callie."

He massaged the tense muscles tightening the back of his neck. The failure of his marriage was still too raw to delve into, even with Livvie. He hadn't shared details with anyone. Not now. Maybe not ever. Part of why he'd avoided seeing his best friends for so long.

"Yeah. Anyway, traveling from California will be a lot easier. And I'm not going to take as many gigs. I'm working on figuring out how to freelance and cut the travel time in half."

But he didn't want to think about the future right now. He wanted to enjoy tonight. "Enough about me. Anything new with librarian life?"

She clapped her hands together, her face lighting up. "Ohmygod, I'm doing some of the coolest stuff right now with special collections. I was waiting to tell you in person but I may have the chance to go to Greece and curate next year."

"Greece? Like Athens or one of the islands?" Greek history and mythology were his jam. Reading helped him stay grounded on the road.

She nodded enthusiastically. "UCSD has partnerships with both public and private collectors. I've got a few different potential options, maybe Crete or Rhodes."

"That's awesome. I know how much you've wanted to travel. Is it for a few weeks or something?" His pulse kicked against his ribs. Damn it, much as he bitched about being on the road too much, the idea of travel always pumped up his adrenaline.

"No, most of the opportunities are for one year. Can you imagine? Me. Finally getting a passport and taking off to see the world." A shadow flickered across her creamy skin. She looked down and sipped her drink.

The three of them had planned on attending separate colleges in New York--something different than their Southern California lifestyle. Seasons and tradition and three thousand miles away from their families. Freedom.

Then in one tragic moment on the ski slopes of Utah, Livvie's mom had been permanently disabled. Instead of flying to New York for university, Livvie became her mom's caretaker. While Grant and Toby spent their twenties traveling the world, Livvie never left San Diego. He'd done his best showing her new locales on their weekly calls, but it wasn't the same.

His gut clenched, but he forced himself to keep his voice light. "You deserve it and it will be amazing. But damn, the timing blows. I'm finally going to live here again and you're leaving. We need to hang out a lot before you go. I've missed you."

She squeezed his hand. "I've missed you too. We can revive the Three Musketeers.

The good old days. Aha, here comes Toby bearing another round."

Toby's generally affable expression was thunderous and he smacked the drinks onto the table.

"Hey, don't shatter the bottles. What's wrong?" Olivia reached for the longneck beer and frowned up at their friend.

He flung himself into the booth. "You remember Blake Carson?" He threw up his hands and plowed on without waiting for a reply. "Well, he's a goddamn flake. He's supposed to do the shoot for my event up in Mammoth over New Year's and just bailed."

"Are you serious? You've had that exhibition scheduled since last year, right?" Olivia's jaw dropped.

Toby slapped the table with his palm. "Damn straight. And I had to pull a ton of strings to get this off the ground. I called in every favor from the snowboarders, the whole damn Mammoth Mountain organization, you name it. They are all doing this for free and now Blake just backs out. Part of the compensation was to give everyone great publicity shots. What the hell am I going to do now?"

After Toby retired early from his snowboarding career, he'd started a charity for disabled athletes. The organization was funded solely through the major events he held in different ski towns each year. Sure, he had sponsors and donations, but the annual event was the primary method of fundraising. Damn.

"Why don't I do it? I'm sure Samantha will give me the time off, knowing it's to help you. Even though the ranch is in busy season, she's got plenty of crew. What's the deal?" He missed wielding his camera and hadn't done a gig since he'd arrived stateside last summer. Bonus for helping out his best friend.

Toby's eyes gleamed. "Dude, that would be awesome. It's an exhibition on New Year's Day––mostly shooting the riders in the morning. Some location shots around the mountain, some lifestyle shots––you know the deal. Nothing over the top."

"I've missed shooting winter sports. Will we have time to board?" A tingle of anticipation shot up Grant's spine.

"Absolutely." Toby nodded. "I was planning on heading up on the thirtieth. I have a big condo there where we can stay. There's a big New Year's Eve party at one of the athlete's houses, the exhibition is on New Year's Day and then come home on the second. And Livvie, you should come too."

Olivia tilted her head toward him. "Like old times?"

Grant's enthusiasm built. Snowboarding and a chance to support Toby? And a return to Mammoth, where they went every chance they got back in high school. Strong athletes, they used to ride from the moment the slopes opened until they were booted off the mountain. "You don't have plans over New Year's, right?"

She rolled her eyes and grinned. "No, I do not. I think it sounds like a fantastic idea. I just dumped the latest Tinder tragedy and I have zero plans."

"Tinder tragedy?"

"I guess you haven't started dating again. Online is a nightmare, but if you're busy, you're kind of stuck with it. The last five guys I met for a drink were disasters. Not even worth discussing." Olivia shuddered and tucked her hair behind her ear.

Toby raised his bottle. "I'll drink to that. And I have a possible New Year's date, so maybe I can delete the app once and for all."

Grant grimaced. Dating? Hell no, he wasn't dating. Not any time in the foreseeable century, if ever. "I'll take your word it. I'm in for Mammoth." Something loosened in his chest. Time away with these two might be just what the doctor ordered.

Olivia reached out and squeezed his forearm and a spark flew up his arm. "I'm sorry. I didn't mean to be flippant about dating."

"I'm fine." He casually slid his arm away from her. What the hell with that jolt when she'd touched him?

Her gaze was speculative, but she simply sipped her beer.

"I'm psyched. You're a lifesaver, Grant, and a hell of a better photographer than that guy anyways. As usual, you two are the ones I can count on--the Three Musketeers are back together. On New Year's Eve, no less." Toby grinned.

Maybe his life was back on track. Mammoth? Stepping behind the camera again, for a good cause, and time with his best friends was the perfect start to his new life.

CHAPTER 2

"Are we there yet?" Olivia knew she sounded like an impatient kid, but somehow, she'd forgotten that every time they drove to Mammoth it took hours longer than she anticipated. Felt like eons. Sure, maybe they'd made it in just under six hours in high school, but these days they'd graduated to driving slower than ninety miles per hour.

"You know it takes almost seven hours and we messed up when we cut through Temecula. The traffic there blows," Toby said.

"Yeah, I'm with Livvie. Can't you drive a little faster, Grandpa?" Grant chimed in from the back seat of Toby's vintage Land Rover.

Toby held up his middle finger in the rearview. "Screw you. Ask our resident mechanic. If I push this baby beyond her limits, she'll break down on me and I'm sure Livvie doesn't want to spend this trip repairing my car."

Olivia sighed. "You told me everything is running smoothly. Grant could have driven." No way did she want to work on Toby's temperamental beast up in the mountains.

Not when they'd had a foot of fresh powder and the temperature was hovering around twenty-nine degrees.

Her 1966 Mustang, although in prime condition, wouldn't appreciate the icy roads. Four-wheel drive wasn't always a requirement up in the Sierra Nevada mountains, but it was the safest option. Besides, with the guys and their snowboards and gear, it would have been a tight squeeze.

"I could have, but Toby insisted. So how is the Mustang?" Grant shifted closer, his broad hands gripping the back of her seat.

"She's looking better than when I got her in high school and wait until you see the stereo I installed. If only we'd had that sound system in high school." Olivia angled her head back and her breath caught in her throat. She snapped her gaze toward the scenery again.

Damn, Grant had always been good-looking, even as a kid. But he'd been like her little brother––he and Toby loved to give her crap that she was and always would be a year older. Like that made her ancient.

Ever since she'd laid her hand on his sinewy forearm at Fidel's, a different type of awareness had arisen within her. An unwelcome one. She nibbled on the inside of her lower lip. It was fine. She just hadn't seen him in person in years and something felt different now.

But he was one of her best friends, not some guy she'd swiped right on for a potential date. Well, hell to the yes, she would have swiped if she saw him as a stranger, but she'd definitely not met anyone like him online or anywhere else. *Anyways.*

Time to tamp down the hormones and pull it together. Grant was her lifelong friend––someone she counted on to be there for her, no matter what. She couldn't jeopardize their relationship because now she couldn't seem to stop ogling him. She intertwined her fingers in her lap and squeezed. *Focus, girl.* She hadn't heard a word he'd uttered.

"Listening to music in your car when we were kids was the best, especially on concert nights. Anyways, ten miles to go. Let me fill you in a little more on the next few days." Toby saved the day by changing the subject.

"Perfect. Can't wait." This was the first weekend away she'd taken in what seemed like forever. Snowboarding, great company, and time to truly catch up with her two best friends sounded like heaven. Emphasis on *friends.*

They had agreed on the trip the night after Thanksgiving, and December had been hectic, to say the least. Many of her colleagues at The Geisel Library at the University of California, San Diego, where she was an archivist librarian, left town en masse over the holidays. Between doing her own work, covering for co-workers who'd taken vacation time, and finishing applications for a few fascinating opportunities abroad, her brain was toast. She'd barely surfaced for a breath and it was already the end of the year.

"Yeah, when do I start officially? Is tomorrow a free day while we board or do you want me to get some lifestyle shots of the athletes? Tell me the deal," Grant said, rubbing his palms together.

"You've got it super easy. I really just need the bulk of the shots on the event day. The riders, the party, all that. Things I can use on the website and share on social to set up for next year," Toby said.

"Awesome. When's the last time we all rode together?" Olivia clapped her hands together.

Grant shook his head. "It's been years since all three of us have managed to get together. The few times I've been back in winter we just couldn't seem to coordinate it. Hell, I haven't seen you in five years, Livvie."

She angled back toward him again, her heart warming. "I

can't believe it's been so long. Once we're together, it always feels like yesterday. I love you guys." Such a gift to be able to slip into a comfortable rhythm, no matter what.

She squeezed his leg and rubbed Toby's broad shoulder. Ignored the sparks from touching Grant. *Damn it.* Grant and Toby had been her best friends––the two people in the world who knew her best. Being an only child with a single mom, they'd been her male influence.

Grant had always had a streak of melancholy. Grant had only been eleven years old when his policeman father had been killed in the line of duty. His mom, Angela, was a strong woman and had assumed the role for both parents for her three sons. Later, she married Chris McNeill, who was a powerful and loving presence, but Grant had never been the same.

When his dad died, Grant got a hollow-eyed look that eventually faded. He had that look now. Last month, in the darkened bar, it hadn't been as obvious. But in the unforgiving December daylight, the violet shadows beneath his eyes were apparent and his usually lean cheeks appeared gaunt. His eyes were an unusual golden amber that usually glowed with warmth, like a lion sunning himself on the savannah.

Today, they resembled the dull bronze of an old penny–– somehow flat. Either he was truly exhausted from his nomadic lifestyle, or the brutal split from Callie had truly shattered his heart. Over the last few years when his marriage was falling apart, he'd refused to discuss it, keeping their calls more focused on work and recreation. Did he still love his wife?

Hopefully Grant wouldn't revert into his usual MO of downplaying his problems and would share what rippled beneath the surface. Olivia had always been the one who could draw him out, so she'd do her best to encourage him to open up this weekend.

"All for one and one for all!" Toby shook a fist in the air. "We'll be eighty years old and cheering each other on. Okay, let's stop at Vons and stock up on some groceries. I want to be set for the next few days. We can walk to the slopes and I'd rather just park the car for the weekend."

"With you on the Three Musketeers forever. I heard there's a storm front coming in tomorrow." Olivia glanced out the window, as always admiring the beauty of this stunning mountain town. The wide roads created a sense of openness, emphasized by the soaring snow-covered mountain peaks, the endless bowl of lavender-streaked twilight sky, framed with enormous spears of evergreens.

She rolled down the window and drank in the crisp— well, okay, bone-chilling—air. "We're not in San Diego anymore, guys. I hope I didn't forget all my long johns. Brrr."

"Roll that up, Hanlon––I don't have my jacket on," Toby barked at her.

"When did you become such a delicate flower?" She pressed the button and the window slid up silently. "I hope you're not going to be complaining all day tomorrow on the slopes like you did that one year." She snorted with laughter.

Grant chuckled. "Oh yeah, the year you forgot your snowboarding pants and tried to ride in jeans. You bitched and moaned like an old lady."

"Hey, it was freezing that day and normally, it wouldn't matter because I never fall, but that beginner came careening down the hill and catapulted me into a tree. I could have died and here you two are mocking me years later. And I'm giving you a free weekend. Should I drop you off at the Motel 6?" Toby raised one ginger brow.

Olivia wiped her eyes. That day had been funny and scary

at the same time. "Come on, Toby, it's just us giving you crap."

"Yeah, since when did you take anything we say seriously?" Grant said.

Toby rolled his moss green eyes and tapped the turn signal, entering the Vons parking lot, the main shopping center in town. Almost all the spaces were filled and the whole place hummed with activity. "I'm not sensitive. Just reminding you not to be a dick. Man, looks like everyone just got off the slopes."

People sporting vivid colored jackets, knit beanies, and sheepskin boots tromped into the market, their cheeks flushed and eyes bright from a day carving through Mammoth's trademark powder. Toby parked and they filed out of the SUV and crossed toward the busy store. Patches of ice dotted the sidewalk, crunching beneath their feet, the crackling sound adding to the buzz of voices.

Grant wrapped an arm around her shoulder and squeezed her close. The heat from his body helped lessen the chill from the dry, wintry air.

She slid her arm around his lean waist. "It's so good to see you. I'm so looking forward to hanging out and catching up."

"Me too. It feels great to be back in the mountains. Okay, let's do this. I'm ready for some whiskey. It's freezing up here." Grant gave an exaggerated shiver.

"I've got some Red Breast 15 in the car, so we're set. I was thinking of grilling some burgers––sound good?" Toby asked and grabbed a cart.

After cruising the aisles and buying enough food to last a family of six an entire week, they were on their way. Toby navigated down the main road and Olivia admired the twinkling lights and alpine architecture of the Village at Mammoth Mountain. An enormous Christmas tree gleamed from the center of the courtyard and people filled the bars and restaurants. New Year's weekend was a popular one at Mammoth, especially with the population from LA and San Diego.

They'd have to hit the slopes early to avoid the crush of tourists and the novices who visited once or twice a year. Not like she'd been on her snowboard for the last few seasons, but she was experienced enough that it was like riding a bike to clip her boots onto her board and ride. She'd loved the snow before her mom's accident. Even though the first few times she'd returned afterwards were frightening, she refused to allow fear to ruin her love for the mountains.

Toby turned right and ascended another curving hill, where each house grew larger than the last.

"Um, thought you said we were in a condo? These are mansions," Grant said.

"Well, they've divided a four-thousand-square-foot A-frame into two condos. We've got the upstairs, which is the bomb, and I assume somebody's down below," Toby said, leaning forward to peer out the windows.

Olivia grinned. "Now we're talking. My place is so small at home, it will be nice to spread out. And the way you two snore, maybe I'll be able to actually get some sleep without wearing earplugs."

Both the guys snored like trumpeting moose if they slept on their backs––something she'd experienced the first time they'd all crashed in Toby's mom's basement when they were thirteen. Well, the guys were twelve and she was thirteen.

"Hey, I only snore when I drink too much," Grant said, pressing a hand to his chest like an outraged Victorian virgin. "So yeah, I'll probably be making some noise."

"I got my deviated septum fixed last year and I sleep silent as a possum," Toby said.

"You got a nose job, man? Seriously?" Grant snickered.

"Hey, not a nose job, asshole. I'm already too handsome. I

don't want to look like a Ken doll like you." Toby bared his teeth at Grant.

"Kids, am I going to have to separate you? Good for you, Toby. Grant can sleep downstairs if he's too loud." She reached over and tapped the end of Toby's long straight nose. It didn't look any different to her.

Toby wasn't what you would call classically handsome. His face was too lean, his chin too sharp, his brows too thick, his shock of orange-red hair too bright. He was medium height and wiry, which served him well on the slopes and in the ocean. His nickname was Fox and women loved him because he was charming and hilarious and had a heart of gold.

Throw in the fact he was a philanthropist and he was practically perfect. Despite growing up with a philandering dad who abandoned his family, Toby always managed to appear lighthearted. But he didn't trust easily. Like her, he was perpetually single.

"Here it is." Toby parked in front of a gorgeous redwood A-frame. He clicked an electronic opener and pulled into the double garage. They piled out of the car, grabbing the groceries and the first round of bags.

When they entered the main floor, Olivia's jaw dropped. "Wow."

Soaring ceilings with windows that filled the far wall framed a postcard view of the snow-covered mountains and darkening evening sky. A huge gray shaker stone fireplace dominated one wall, with a sprawling olive-green L-shape sofa inviting them to lounge. The other side of the great room consisted of a huge kitchen boasting a granite island with leather barstools, a gleaming stainless steel hood over a gas range, and a white subway-tiled backsplash.

"Awesome." Toby dropped the groceries on the counter and hurried to the French doors leading to an enormous deck. "And check out the grill and hot tub, which sounds like the perfect plan for tonight. You guys ready for cocktails and burgers?"

"Definitely. I'll grab the rest of the bags." Grant headed back to the garage.

"I'd say your friend totally styled us out. I'm going to pick my room. Did you say there's one down here and two upstairs?" Olivia asked.

"Yeah. Let's take the upstairs rooms so if he sounds like a charging rhino tonight, we won't hear him." Toby smirked and started to pull food out of the grocery bags.

"Do you need help with that?"

"Nah, go pick your room. Burgers are my specialty so I got it covered." He flicked a hand in the air.

"You don't have to tell me twice." Olivia grinned, grabbed her duffle bag, and bounded up the stairs.

Her heart sang. The new chapter in her life was unfolding, beginning with eating, drinking, and snowboarding with Toby and Grant. Sometimes it felt like she'd skipped the carefree twenties and gone from teenager to adult overnight. No more. Now that her aunt had moved in with her mom, Olivia could finally explore the world beyond San Diego. Next year, she would head off to Greece, and finally be able to live her dreams instead of experiencing them vicariously through her friends and her beloved books.

And in the midst of all the revelry, she'd get to the bottom of why Grant's brooding side seemed to be dominant and make sure her friend felt better by the time they returned.

CHAPTER 3

Grant slammed the door shut and dropped the rest of the gear onto the taupe hardwood floors. He'd unloaded their snowboards into the locker in the garage. When he entered the kitchen, Toby was pouring three glasses of Red Breast 15 into matching glass tumblers.

"Starting with the whiskey. Perfect." Grant chose one, but before he sipped, looked around. "Where's Olivia?"

Toby closed the bottle and picked up the two remaining drinks. "Upstairs. Your room is down here--the door on the other side of the fireplace."

"Wait for me." Olivia flew down the stairs, her long dark hair floating around her shoulders, her enormous ocean-blue eyes wide. "We've got to start our trip off with a toast."

"We wouldn't dare start without you." Grant grinned at the urgency in her tone. Same old Olivia--never wanted to miss a moment--one of her most endearing traits. Damn, was it good to see her.

Toby stepped forward and handed her the whiskey. "Cheers to the Three Musketeers back together again. Mammoth won't know what hit it this weekend."

The glasses clinked, chiming like a clear peal of a ringing bell. Grant tasted his drink and savored the nutty flavor exploding on his tongue. "Now that is some fine whiskey. Haven't tried Red Breast before."

"You know me, a man of impeccable taste." Toby swept his arm overhead in one of his trademark dramatic gestures. "Now I'm starving and am going to fire up the grill. Olivia—you slice the tomatoes and lettuce and prep the condiments. Grant—you build us a big-ass fire. Deal?" He turned and headed to the deck without waiting for a reply.

Grant and Olivia stared at each other a moment and burst out laughing. "I swear he was Caesar in a past life. Lucky for him we're always on the same page."

"Building a fire is the least I can do for this sweet pad and weekend. I needed this." Something softened in Grant's chest.

His family was great, but his older brother Ryan was only arriving back in California next month and Austin was still in New York. In the months since Grant had arrived stateside, Toby had been traveling and Olivia working nonstop. Their schedules hadn't meshed until last month. He resolved to make sure they hung out more.

Olivia tilted her head and her eyes narrowed. "You bought the groceries too, don't forget. Are you okay, Grant? I mean, really okay? I know you've been holding back on me this past year. I didn't want to push, but I'm here."

Grant stiffened for a moment and forced his shoulders to unwind. "I will be. It's been a hell of a year and I didn't want to drag you down. I'll figure it out." *I sure as hell hope I can figure it out...*

She stepped up and hugged him. "Well, it is almost the New Year and that's always symbolic for a fresh start. Every-thing can change in the blink of an eye and you can always talk to me."

His arms came around her and he rested his chin on her silky dark hair. Damn, she smelled delicious. Her breasts were crushed against him and suddenly this wasn't his best friend, but a gorgeous, desirable woman in his arms. He jerked back.

"Grant?" Her eyes widened, hurt gleaming in their depths. Oblivious to the fact that now he was sporting a hard-on. He turned and sprinted to the fireplace, out of her proximity. What the hell?

"All good. Just don't want to get in trouble with Toby." He laughed when he saw it was a gas fireplace, so no actual fire-building involved. Hopefully she hadn't noticed the major issue in his pants.

She huffed and retreated to the kitchen. "Whatever. But don't think you can hide from me this weekend. Something's going on and you'll tell me eventually. You always do."

Of course, she was correct. Olivia had always been the person he could confide in and their ability to share their emotions and experiences with each other was the pillar of their deep connection. But this wasn't like confiding about losing his dad or screwing up a job.

No, he'd been aroused by her presence and that was new. Sure, over the years there'd been a couple of times where they'd had a few…moments. Considered each other. She was hot. But she was his friend and that superseded anything else. So any time he'd ever felt any type of spark around her, he swiftly extinguished it.

If he'd learned one thing over these past years, it was that he needed friends he could trust. True friends. And he couldn't go messing up his closest friendship because he was horny.

Toby burst back into the room. "You guys are gonna die when you get a load of that Jacuzzi. We could have a dozen people in there." He sauntered into the kitchen and grabbed the burgers.

"Tell me there aren't a dozen people coming over." Olivia groaned and pointed the sharp knife at Toby.

Toby laughed and shook his head. "Nope. Just us tonight and then we've got that party tomorrow. But if any of us meet someone tomorrow night, there's room." He waggled his ginger eyebrows.

Olivia poked Toby in the shoulder. Thankfully not with the knife. "That was fast. Three Musketeers is now hot tub sex party. No way."

"Yeah, man, c'mon." The last thing Grant wanted to see was Olivia's taut little body all slick and slippery and cozied up to some random dude in the hot tub. And again, where did that visual come from?

Toby held up his hands. "Full disclosure. There's a chick who's going to be at the party tomorrow night and I'm hoping to hang with her. But I could always go to her place if it's a problem."

"Of course it isn't a problem. You just made it sound like you wanted some big party here, and I'd rather spend quality time with you two. But if you like this girl, that's fine with me." Olivia returned to chopping.

Toby shrugged. "Her name is Erin--she's cool. She works for Burton. We met once and I'm hoping my charm and good looks will win her over."

"Don't they always?" Grant slapped his buddy on the back.

"Very true. Okay, I'm toasting the buns and adding cheddar unless I hear different. I'd also dig some of that Paso Robles GSM blend unless you guys want beer?"

Olivia was already rifling through drawers. "I'm definitely in the mood for red wine up here in the mountains. But I'll pour us all water, so we don't succumb to the altitude too fast." She whipped out a corkscrew and turned to grab the wine bottle.

And had she always had a perfect heart-shaped ass or was he losing his damn mind tonight? He needed some frigid fresh air. Pronto.

"I'll help with the burgers." Grant snatched up the buns and jogged after Toby. Time to screw his head on straight before he did something idiotic. Like hit on his best friend and ruin that relationship too.

TOBY BELCHED and rubbed his belly. "Now those burgers were spectacular, if I do say so myself."

"I'm so glad your modest side hasn't changed at all." Grant laughed and rolled his eyes at Olivia.

"You're right though––best cheeseburger ever. I cannot wait to hit the fresh powder from the storm earlier this week, although I hope we get a bluebird weekend, all sunshine, no more snow." Olivia leaned back in her chair and sipped her wine.

"It's supposed to be epic, like the snow always is up here. And there's another storm rolling in. You'll be okay, right, Livvie?" Toby's brows rose.

She nodded. "I can handle a snowstorm. I'd just prefer sunshine."

Grant double-checked and her expression was serene. After her mom's accident, he'd worried Livvie wouldn't return to the mountains. "What time are we heading over?"

"Let's plan on eight? We can get a full day, come back and chill in the Jacuzzi and have plenty of time before the New Year's Eve party. Cool?" Toby asked.

"Perfect. I'm going to change and go in the hot tub. I'm all stiff from the drive and need to loosen my muscles. Join me?" Olivia stood, her rosy lips curved up.

"Well, you are the oldest, so I guess that arthritis is beginning to kick in? Bifocals next? Osteoporosis?" Toby joked.

She stuck out her tongue. "Please. One year does not a senior make. Will the day ever come where you two don't give me crap because I'm a mere year older?"

Grant stood. "Never. And I'm with you. My lower back is screaming. Meet you outside in five." *When you're already submerged in the water and I don't have to see all that creamy bare skin.*

"Welcome to our thirties. I'll pour us some more Red Breast and meet you out there." Toby dumped his plate in the sink and reached for the whiskey.

Grant went to his assigned room and tossed his duffle bag on the king-size bed––damn, did he really snore that loud or were they just giving him shit? Callie had never mentioned it, so maybe he'd outgrown it or something? Not that there was anyone around to sleep with him these days.

The bedroom was huge and the far wall was a sheet of glass, just like the main room. Pretty sweet. Even in the darkness, the snow decorated the enormous evergreens like frosting on a cake, the jagged peaks of the Sierras perched behind them. A dusting of clouds hinted at the snow to fall the next day, which he was looking forward to. He couldn't remember the last time he'd been in the snow. Switzerland? The Andes? Whistler?

This weekend was the perfect getaway to remind him that he didn't have to fly halfway across the world for a total change of scenery.

He shook his head and unzipped the bag, yanking out his stuff and tossing it on the chocolate brown velvet comforter. There they were––his favorite board shorts. He hadn't been kidding about his back aching. He'd injured it surfing Byron

Bay a few years ago and now when the weather was cold, it tended to flare up.

Like an old man––sometimes he felt decades older than thirty-two. He'd played hard and fast with his body since he was a kid. He never felt more free than when he was in the zone surfing or boarding or pushing himself physically. But these days, he had to be more careful. Like an old man.

No use ruminating over it. He was young and healthy and simply needed the scorching water to set himself right. And some more whiskey wouldn't hurt. He tossed his clothes on the floor, pulled on his shorts, and grabbed a hoodie. Hopefully Olivia was already immersed chin deep. Safer that way.

He strode through the living room and out the French doors to the deck. The glacial wind slammed into him like a brick wall and he sucked in a breath.

Tinkling laughter came from the massive Jacuzzi. "Freezing, right? We are not used to this weather. Hurry, shut the door and hop in with us." Only Olivia's head and gleaming pale shoulders were visible above the bubbling water. Thank god.

He jogged up the steps to pull himself over the edge and slid into the water. He hissed through his teeth as the gurgling liquid seared his skin. "Whoa. We're going to boil like a bunch of lobsters in here." He grabbed the rim and held himself half-in and half-out of the hot tub.

"You'll get used to it." Olivia sipped her drink, her eyes sweeping across his bare chest and arms. "Wow. You're ripped, Grant."

On reflex, he found himself puffing out his chest like a damn rooster. He couldn't discern the expression on her face, but even in the dim light her eyes sparkled. Her hair was piled on top of her head in one of those messy topknots, which somehow made her look even sexier. Her cheeks were pink and her lips parted. Was that what she looked like when she orgasmed?

"You been hitting the gym or something?" Toby offered him a plastic solo cup and effectively doused the dangerous direction of Grant's musings.

He accepted the drink and settled into the hot tub. Time to snap back to how it always was——platonic. Pronto. If she'd stay submerged, maybe he could get a grip.

"Grant?" Olivia's brows rose.

"Sorry. It took a minute to adjust to this water." He leaned against the smooth Jacuzzi wall, positioning himself in front of one of the pulsating jets. "Yeah, I've been working with Sam on the ranch and it's a lot of physical labor. And I've been practicing some Brazilian ju-jitsu with my brother-in-law Holt."

"Well, it looks good on you. My best friends are the hottest dudes in town." Olivia's tone was light, but the intensity in her eyes lingered.

If she'd been any other woman, Grant would've sworn she was flirting with him. Maybe he wasn't the only one experiencing a shift in perspective. And what would that even mean?

"Well, you're smokin' hot, sweetheart. Are you open to meeting some of the athletes this weekend? I've got a couple guys who might be worthy of you." Toby quirked a brow.

"Dude, what's with the setups? I thought this weekend was for the three of us." Grant pointed to the Three Muske-teers tattoo on his inner left wrist.

"Yeah, it's supposed to be the Three Musketeers weekend, Toby. I mean, I thought we agreed. Or you just don't want to feel guilty abandoning us when you meet up with that girl?" Olivia frowned and gestured with her tattooed arm.

Grant nodded vigorously. "What she said. No worries if

you want to hang out with someone, but my divorce isn't even final yet."

"Oh geez, it isn't? Haven't you been back for six months?" Olivia's brows lifted.

Grant shrugged, his mood plummeting. "Yeah. In Melbourne, you've got to be separated for a year first, then you start the formal process, which I did about six months ago. It's close to being official. And I'd rather not talk about it."

He didn't want to burden anyone with his baggage. The last thing he needed was to hash out how bad he'd screwed up his marriage. He hadn't been an ideal husband, at least for a woman wanting a white picket fence and two-point-five kids. Maybe if he'd tried to tame his schedule when Callie had asked, instead of always being eager to take off, things would have worked out differently.

Olivia stared at him for a moment, then flashed a mischievous smile. "Okay, so no random setups, no discussion of breakups. Point taken. In the interest of changing the subject, Toby's bossiness reminded me of that time in tenth grade how his plan to go camping got us all grounded for a month."

"Hey, we planned that together. And it wasn't my fault your mom locked the windows and you couldn't sneak back in your house." Toby laughed.

"Yeah, and then she called our moms after she heard us trying to break into the back door. Lucky for me my mom had just gotten remarried and was in a good mood." Grant's lips twitched.

"At least we never got caught skipping school." Olivia raised her cup.

Toby laughed and waved his tattooed arm. "Right? All for one and one for all. Love you guys and stoked for this weekend. Thanks for coming up."

"Cheers to that." Grant tossed back the smooth whiskey, savoring the burn streaking down his throat.

The next few days were for exhausting his body on the slopes and shutting down the unwelcome memories of his destroyed marriage. Oh yeah, and obliterating this burgeoning attraction to his friend. He couldn't afford to lose anyone else in his life.

Especially Olivia.

CHAPTER 4

Olivia's breath puffed out in short bursts as she approached the base of the St. Anton run. Guns n' Roses "Paradise City" blared through her earbuds. She skidded to a stop and turned to locate Grant. She raised her goggles and glanced up at the giant snowflakes pouring from the sky. A few hours ago, light flurries swirled in the air, but now the frosty flakes were dumping, the arctic wind churning them around.

Some people loved boarding in a "whiteout" situation, but not her. The snowstorms triggered memories she'd prefer to keep buried. It was a wonder she even went to the mountains anymore. Strapped on her board. The ski accident that had rendered her mom a paraplegic occurred during an avalanche. She'd used a wheelchair ever since. That avalanche had not just forever altered her mom's life but had abruptly torn her own life plan apart.

Hell, she usually only went out on bluebird days with glaring sunshine and nonexistent wind. She was a San Diegan through and through.

The single blue thing she could discern in this opaque

gray-white sky was the royal navy of Grant's jacket as he gracefully carved his way to where she waited. His broad shoulders and lean frame were discernable, despite his bulky clothes. He'd always been lithe and strong on the slopes, making the double diamond black run look like a bunny hill. He caught some air and rode up to her side.

Damn, last night when he'd paused halfway into the Jacuzzi, the square shape of his pecs and carved triceps had looked too delicious to resist. Her mouth had watered and she thanked the dim light for hiding her over-the-top reaction to her bestie. Like if she'd leaned over and licked his flat pink nipple it wouldn't have ruined twenty years of friendship.

And why was she noticing him this way now? Sure, he was gorgeous and she appreciated beauty in all forms. But the few instances when she'd felt attraction flare, she'd tucked it away. No way could she afford to lose him or Toby. Between caring for her mom and finishing college and graduate school, she hadn't had much time for making new friends. And nobody could approach the profound connection of the Three Musketeers.

He shoved his goggles up onto the top of his silver helmet and squinted those amber eyes at her. "You done?

She pulled out her earbuds and nodded. "My legs are toast and you know I hate boarding in a storm. Should we wait for Toby?"

Toby had glided off to back country with a few of the pro riders after they'd met up for grilled cheese sandwiches at the Melt House. Olivia wasn't about to blow out her knee attempting to keep up with that crew. She was no novice, but she wasn't that level. Grant was talented enough but had chosen to hang with her.

He spread his arms wide and shook his head. "Who knows. That Jacuzzi is calling my name. You ready?"

She flipped down her goggles. "Absolutely."

They cruised down to the bottom at a leisurely pace. Olivia stopped and unclipped her boots from her lavender and yellow board. Grant unhooked from his and together they crunched across the deepening snow toward the shuttle bus. The bitter wind picked up with each freezing gust, rendering her cheeks practically numb.

They lucked out and the shuttle pulled up right as they reached the curb in the Mammoth Mountain village. Because of the blizzard, people were pouring off the mountain like salmon swimming upstream. The lift kept operating despite what appeared to be a whiteout developing on the top of the mountain. A boisterous group piled into the bus, jostling Olivia into Grant and almost knocking them over. He caught her by the waist before she tumbled them both onto the blackened wet floor.

Even through her layers of silk long underwear, Smartwool sweater, Patagonia board pants, and ski jacket, his broad hands burned into her as if his long fingers were imprinted into her bare skin. She managed not to yelp or act like a total loon while her hands gripped his shoulders to steady herself.

She gazed up and his sculpted beautiful lips were mere inches from her own. The warmth of his breath brushed her cheek and his pupils flared when his gaze met hers. His hands tightened for a split second before he stepped back, breaking the moment.

Oh my god. Now they were having *moments*.

She lightly smacked his shoulder and forced a laugh. "That would figure--first day on the mountain in a few years without a hint of wiping out and then hitting the bus floor."

His gaze grew quizzical for a moment and then cleared. "Right? But don't worry, I wouldn't let you fall."

Something warmed in her chest and she stared out the hazy bus window at the darkening horizon. He'd always been so protective of her. She'd been raised by her single mom and having Toby and Grant stand up for her like brothers had been an integral part of her teenage years. A vital part.

The shuttle let them off at the base of the hill where they were staying. Luckily, their snowboarding boots boasted strong treads, so they trekked up the white sidewalks without incident.

"We don't have to drive to the party tonight, right?" The slick roads and nonstop snow unsettled her stomach.

Grant crouched down, punched in the lockbox code, and retrieved the house key. "Nope. Pretty sure it is just a few blocks away, so we can walk."

He unlocked the door and they dumped their equipment in the attached garage. On the way into the kitchen, Olivia peeled off the protective layers down to her black long underwear top and board pants.

A lovely framed mirror exposed the not-so-lovely after effects of the day. An angry pink welt from her helmet adorned her forehead. She looked awful, her sweaty hair escaping from her French braid, forming a frizzy halo around her blotchy face. She brushed at her bangs, but they remained erect, refusing to cooperate. A snow bunny she was not.

Grant stood with his head stuck in the stainless steel refrigerator. "You ready for a beer for the Jacuzzi?"

Olivia grimaced at her reflection in the mirror. Pondered her physical reaction to him this trip. Without Toby there to balance them out, perhaps getting semi-naked right now with Grant might not be prudent. "Umm, not yet. I need a shower. It always blows me away how sweaty I get boarding when it is freezing outside. I'll be down in a little bit."

"Hey, we have a few hours before the party. You sure you don't want to join?" Grant cracked open a beer.

"Just feel like a shower, that's all." She gave an airy wave and crossed to the stairs. "See you in a little bit." Yes, she was acting kind of weird. Wasn't she the one who said she wanted to spend as much time as possible with him and Toby this weekend?

But she hadn't anticipated the lust curling deep in her belly every time she came within a foot of Grant.

THE EXTENDED STEAMY shower went a long way to clearing Olivia's short-circuiting brain. She'd rationalized this newfound awareness of the sheer physical potency of her best friend. She hadn't dated much over the last decade. And when she had, she was always attracted to the tragic guys who needed some type of saving––good girls and bad boys and all that.

Maybe Grant's difficult divorce was rendering him more attractive––the extra layer of melancholy lent him a sexy rock star air.

She huffed out a breath. Enough ruminating. She smoothed down her hair she'd actually taken the time to dry and throw in a few loose barrel curls, even though they'd probably be destroyed when they walked to the party—hat or no. Whatever. There was something therapeutic about getting ready. She'd done a smoky eye––sure they were in the mountains, but it was New Year's Eve, right?

She slid the silver off-shoulder cashmere sweater over her head, savoring the cotton-candy softness. Yup, she'd chosen wisely for a cold NYE bash. Off the shoulder so she wouldn't look too much like the buttoned-up librarian cliché, but warm and cozy too. Black leather leggings and her combat boots would ensure she didn't wind up spilling on her ass like she and Grant almost had on the shuttle.

She dabbed on some pinky nude gloss, perfect for a night she was sure would be full of cocktails, and headed downstairs in her wool socks. It was only six and they weren't heading over to the party for another hour or two. They'd eat dinner in the house before braving the snowstorm. The sky was milky pale now, the dark and stars completely shrouded beneath the storm. Part of her wished they could just stay in, dance to the killer playlists she'd thrown together for the trip, and reminisce about the good old days.

The glory days of the Three Musketeers. The days in junior high and high school, when they had been inseparable. From hours listening to music in Toby's basement, to catching waves every chance they had, to the guys standing up to the mean kids who'd made fun of Livvie's four-eyes and brace face. They'd always supported each other through the crises and shared the best times.

Nothing turned out like their grand plans to conquer New York and explore the world together. Toby toured internationally as an elite pro snowboarder. Grant zigzagged the globe photographing the international sports scene. And after her mom's accident, she'd delayed school for a year and become her full-time caretaker, never leaving San Diego. She'd completed undergrad at UCSD, then earned her Master's in Library Science from the San Jose State online program.

Even when the guys had managed to be in town simultaneously, they often popped in without warning and she'd been unable to see them unless they came to see her and her mom.

Luckily, they had the kind of friendship where you could not talk for a few months and then pick up where you left off. Easy. Simple. Profound. Rare.

She skipped down the stairs, affection filling her veins and heart. She loved these guys. They were family. They'd have a blast tonight and she'd make sure to spend as much time as possible with them over the next couple of months before she went to Greece.

Probably went to Greece. No, she shook her head. Definitely went to Greece––she'd accepted a position. Nothing would change her mind––she'd devoted her twenties to her mom. Now it was her turn to travel and find adventure abroad.

Raucous laughter greeted her. Toby and Grant were doubled over the edge of the kitchen island, both of them shaking with hilarity.

"What's so funny? Let me in on the joke." She strolled over and smacked Toby on the back.

He straightened and gave a wolf whistle. "Well hello, heartbreaker. Damn, you clean up good, little girl."

She fluffed her hair and smiled back. "Why thank you. And make up your mind. Am I a little girl or an old lady?" In her sock-clad feet she was a shrimp compared to the guys.

Grant was staring at her, his eyes narrowed. "You look amazing." His lighthearted tone didn't match the intensity gleaming in his molten gold eyes.

"Oh, stop, you two. You're just used to seeing me as one of the guys. It's only a little makeup." A flush crept into her cheeks. Grant hadn't stopped staring at her like she was a mouthwatering dessert he'd like to sample.

Grant shoved away from the counter. "I'm going to hit the shower. Wait for me to pop the Veuve." He strode to his room.

Through iron willpower, if she did say so herself, Olivia managed not to stare after him. He had a towel wrapped around his lean waist, and his perfect tapered V-shaped back glistened from the Jacuzzi. Whew. So much for her resolution to look at him like her bestie. She turned back to Toby--thank god he still looked like her friend.

"I got us three bottles of Veuve and I just stuck a pizza from Giovanni's in the oven to warm up for dinner." Toby grinned. "Figured we'd fill up before tonight."

"Three bottles? One each?"

"Nah, we've got a couple more nights. The party is open bar, but we at least want one bottle before we go, right? And if I can talk Erin into coming back here with me tonight, there may be some champagne in the hot tub." He winked.

Olivia laughed. Toby was the flirtatious lighthearted one of their trio. "So, is she serious or just a hookup?"

Toby's face sobered. "She's not a hookup. She's cool and lives in San Diego. But we haven't gone out yet."

"New Year's Eve is filled with a lot of expectations, right? Don't break her heart."

"Hey, I'm not a heartbreaker. Remember I was on the tour circuit forever and that's not conducive to serious relationships. I don't lead anybody on. And my 'one lie, you're gone' policy weeds them out fast."

She stepped in and gave him a one-armed hug. Nope, zero sparks with *this* best friend. "I know you aren't. But you're thirty-two now and maybe it's time to find the one."

"Hey, you're thirty-three." He held up three fingers on each hand. "And you're not married either. And after the way Grant looks these days, I'm not sure marriage appeals."

"True. I'm a little worried he hasn't opened up yet." Olivia tucked a strand of hair behind her ear. "And I still need to see the world before I settle down. You deserve an awesome woman, Toby."

"Aww, getting sentimental? He'll talk when he's ready. Let's just have a good time with the people who we love best. And maybe Erin, if I bring her back." He flashed his wolfish grin.

"Go take a shower, stinky. If you're going to charm this woman, it would help if you smelled better." She pinched her nose and stepped over to the refrigerator.

"You're a riot, Hanlon, a regular riot." Toby lifted an arm and sniffed his armpit. "And you are correct. I do stink. Can't wait to tell you guys about this backcountry area we rode."

"I'm always right, a fact you should be accustomed to after all these years. I'm going to make a salad. You want some, right?" She pulled out the bagged arugula, a cucumber, a carrot and some celery.

"Definitely. Thanks for putting that together. I'll be back in a few."

Olivia walked over to the fireplace where she'd left her purse and her phone. She linked into the Bluetooth and started the '90s grunge playlist she'd created for tonight. She figured they'd start out with a vintage list before the party, where they'd be sure to play dance music.

In high school, they had attended concerts together every chance they could, usually cruising in her Mustang, music blaring. They shared an affinity for the poignant rock that emerged before they were born. Alice in Chains blared through the surround speakers the house boasted. She started prepping the salad, swaying her hips to the soulful music. Being with her best friends made her emotional.

It wasn't that she didn't have other friends, nor was she shy, but like the guys, she was just particular who she let close to her. Her alone time was precious.

"This song brings me back."

Olivia whirled and her breath lodged in her throat. Grant's chestnut hair was still damp and slicked away from his face, highlighting his chiseled cheekbones and square jaw. He wore a long-sleeved black Henley that clung to his broad chest and lean frame. Dark jeans hugged his narrow hips and long legs. Altogether, he was a devastating sight.

"You ready for me to pop the cork?" He angled his head to the side, his brows raised. "Livvie?"

She snapped back to attention. "Sorry. I think the altitude is getting to me. I feel a little lightheaded."

He covered the space between them in two long strides and clasped her shoulders. "Are you okay? Do you want me to get you something to eat or do you need aspirin?" Concern etched along his forehead and his long amber eyes narrowed.

She managed not to jolt at the touch of his calloused palms searing into her bare skin but couldn't halt the tingling of her nerves. Shit shit *shit.* Her visceral reaction confirmed she had a major problem. In the past, they had hugged and touched without her wanting to jump his bones.

Now, she was hot for her best friend. And she needed to break the spell.

She inhaled an unsteady breath and retreated a step, then hurried around him toward the refrigerator. "I'm fine. You know if I don't eat every three hours my blood sugar plummets. And the day on the mountain took it out of me. The pizza should be ready, but maybe I need a snack."

And she was babbling. She yanked open the fridge and pulled out the celery, carrots, and cucumber she'd arranged on a tray for them last night. Maybe he wouldn't notice.

"You're acting weird. But maybe I've just forgotten that part of your personality. I'll open the champagne." Grant brushed by her, the heat from his body scorching her. His voice was neutral.

"You know me. Dorky four-eyed Olivia." The guys used to handle the bullies who had teased her for the thick glasses she used to wear before she got Lasik.

"Your glasses made you look like a librarian. Which now you are. So you don't have to wear them at all anymore?"

"For reading I do. Once I started working on my master's,

all the studying got to me. But I'm great with distance now, which is amazing. You know I couldn't ever handle contacts." They'd driven her bananas.

"Makes sense." He nodded at her. Then, he turned and bellowed up the stairs, "Toby get your ass in here, I'm popping the cork now."

And just like that, there he was: her platonic friend Grant. Maybe that's all it took to jolt her back to reality--his yelling like an obnoxious teen boy. The sexy guy tempting her to stroke her hands along his lithe body was just her buddy again.

The danger of crossing the forbidden friendship barrier had disappeared.

For now.

CHAPTER 5

They half-skated, half-stumbled along the slippery-ass frozen sidewalk to the New Year's Eve party. Toby and Livvie were debating the best snowboarding movie of all time. Despite the frigid wind and falling snow, Grant's heart was warm. His best friends had that effect on him. For as long as he could remember, he'd always been restless. Just part of his nature. After his dad was killed in the line of duty, his craving for the next adrenaline rush only amplified.

To feed it, in New York, he and Toby had boarded regularly at Bristol Mountain, where he'd discovered his passion for sports photography. Then, he lucked into an opportunity to go to the Olympic Winter Games in Whistler in 2010 as an apprentice. Boom! That was it. One industry connection led to another, and another, and somehow his life morphed into a whirlwind of pro tours and X-Games and nonstop action. He never went home.

Not really, anyways. He'd parlay the gigs--do lifestyle or brand shoots around the events. When he met Callie and they moved to her hometown of Melbourne, Australia, it was the first time he'd actually planted roots since he'd left California.

And that grand experiment was an utter failure.

"Earth to Grant," Toby howled in his ear.

Grant shook himself back to present. "Sorry. Just thinking how glad I am to be hanging with you two knuckleheads."

"Hey, we are musketeers, not knuckleheads. Get the title right please." Olivia bubbled with laughter and squeezed his arm.

Like they'd done a million times before, they walked arm in arm. But unlike any prior stroll, awareness prickled between him and Livvie. Damn it, with just a small tug of his arm, he could turn her into his body, wrap his arms around her, and capture her full pouty mouth. He inched away and shifted his focus to the surroundings.

The snow poured from the sky and everything from the soaring evergreens to the houses was buried like cake under a thick layer of vanilla frosting. The wind bit into his cheeks and he sucked in a deep breath, trying to cool down the heat that now simmered whenever he was next to Olivia.

Not his objectively pretty friend. F-R-I-E-N-D. Not a hookup. Not someone to date. Time to screw his head on straight. Now he was in San Diego full-time, he needed the Three Musketeers, Version 2.0. He could count on one hand the people he trusted and truly had a great time with, no matter what they did.

Until he got his life in order, he couldn't afford to jeopardize the friendship that offered him the most stability. Everyone knew sex messed up a friendship.

"Only got one more block." Toby pointed down the street, as if they could see a damn thing through the blizzard.

"How can you even tell where we're going?" Grant asked.

"It's super easy. We just walked down the hill from our place and seven blocks east."

Olivia groaned. "You know I hate when you use directions that way. Because in a snowstorm at night in the mountains, I'll be able to tell which way is east."

Toby laughed. "I know, you can only tell directions if the ocean is beside you. Just remember that on the way home, it is seven blocks and then you turn right. Our place is the fifth house on the right. You know, just in case we don't go home at the same time."

"Aha, did you hear from your girlfriend?" Olivia pounced.

"Not my girlfriend. But yeah, Erin texted. She's already there. Hey, and she brought her best friend, who happens to be single." Toby leaned past Olivia and winked at Grant.

Olivia's fingers tightened on his forearm, but then relaxed. Had he imagined her reaction?

"Dude, seriously. I told you. Not interested. Divorce isn't final yet and I just want to hang with you guys." His buddy needed to stop.

"What if Olivia wants to hookup?" Toby challenged.

"Hey, I'm with Grant. Came to hang with my boys." Olivia elbowed Toby hard enough that he stumbled.

"Fine. The party's going to be a blast. Can you hear the music?"

Pumping bass wafted through the frigid air and another A-frame mountain cabin sparkling with lights came into view across the street. Dancing bodies were visible through the enormous front windows, even with the thick snow swirling.

"And we're half a block away still. Wow." Was every person in Mammoth at this party tonight? For some reason, Grant had assumed it would be more casual.

"Yeah, I told you it would be a rager. It'll be a blast, you'll see." Toby quickened his pace and they matched his stride.

"I'll just be happy to be warm and out of this snow. It doesn't look like it's stopping anytime soon." Olivia shivered.

"Staying warm won't be a problem. C'mon, we'll go in and I'll introduce you to Scott--it's his place and he and a few of the other guys are hosting." Toby didn't knock, just pushed the door open.

The music blasted out the door on a wave of steamy air. The crowd surged and Olivia stumbled back, almost tumbling them both off the icy front porch. His arms wrapped around her, and he managed to keep them from falling. And another instant erection, just like on the shuttle bus. He released her the second he confirmed she was steady on her feet.

But he was anything but steady.

"Thanks. Didn't expect that." Olivia laughed and angled her head toward him, her azure eyes sparkling with laughter. "I guess we'll be ringing in the new year in style."

Before he could respond, Toby waved at them. "C'mon. There's a clear path to the bar. Follow me."

They filed in behind him and sure enough, there was space around the perimeter of party central. Thundering music combined with loud conversations assaulted his ears. There had to be a few hundred people packed into the main room, with a tiny stage in the corner and a DJ spinning tunes. It smelled like sweat, pine trees, and fun.

There was enough heat pumping from the gyrating dancers that they could have the fogged-up floor to ceiling windows open and it would still be humid. Flames crackled in the enormous stone fireplace--what rocket scientist had lit a fire tonight?

Grant blew out a breath. Okay, he'd need to find a quieter spot in the house because no way was he going to be crushed to death in the one-hundred-degree room. The muscles in his neck tensed and he struggled to rekindle his good mood.

Damn it, between reminiscing about his failed marriage and lusting after his best friend, he was a mess. Part of him wanted to head back to their place and chill, but it was New Year's Eve and he did want to celebrate a fresh start.

He just didn't know he would want *her* like this.

He was in major trouble.

He followed Toby and Olivia, weaving through the swaying crowd. Thank god her coat was long and covered her down to her knees. Maybe it would be better if they kept on their jackets after all. He ground his teeth together. Self-control had never been an issue and he wasn't going to lose that too.

Tonight he would drink and celebrate with his friends.

Tomorrow he'd be in his element shooting the charity event.

He could handle himself. No problem.

CHAPTER 6

Olivia remained glued to Toby's side and endeavored to control her erratic pulse. When she'd fallen into Grant's powerful arms, every nerve ending in her body leapt to attention. And Grant's raging hard-on pressing against her back had been impossible to miss.

They'd shared a moment. Again. Damn, she'd almost shimmied her hips against him. It had obviously been too long since she'd had sex. Was this new attraction crackling between them the reason he hadn't confided in her yet?

Even after their fun day riding the mountain and sharing dinner and champagne, his tawny eyes remained unreadable. His stillness deeper. She'd always been the one who could reach him when melancholy cloaked his shoulders like darkness descending in a moonless sky.

The one to make him laugh. The one who could sit with him and simply by her presence rescue him from whatever demons troubled him. In fact, she'd always prided herself on being the person who understood him best. Just as she was the one who "got" him, he'd been the same for her.

But right now, he was as enigmatic to her as he usually appeared to other people. And she hated it.

This weekend was about having fun, but also a chance to truly catch up. Despite the attraction shimmering between them, helping Grant heal from his devastating divorce was a priority. She'd accepted her dream job in Crete and would be leaving in March, so ripping his clothes off probably wasn't the smartest move. Being a shoulder he could lean on was the right thing to do.

They reached the bar. Time to simply enjoy a New Year's Eve party, a night of carefree revelry.

"Beer or wine?" Toby tapped her shoulder. He'd carved out a spot at the makeshift bar. "Pay attention, kids. I need to order for us."

"Red wine for me." Sticking with one alcohol for the evening seemed wise.

"I'll take a beer," Grant said as he reached for the chilled bottle.

The hair prickled on the back of her neck when he brushed against her. Again.

She took a fortifying breath and stepped back, creating a miniscule amount of space between them. Toby handed her a plastic cup filled to the brim with beautiful burgundy wine.

"Hey, I see Erin. Will you take our coats back to the coat check? Then come meet her." Toby pointed toward the far end of the great room.

"Oooh, where is she?" Yes, a distraction. But now she'd be alone with Grant. *Crap.*

"She's the blonde in the red sweater over by the far windows. See ya in a few." Toby shoved his jacket at Grant and zipped away.

Grant's lips twitched. "Never seen him so eager. This should be interesting."

"Right? Now do we play it nice or fill her in on some of his best secrets?" She cracked up.

"Nah, it's New Year's Eve. If they end up dating, we'll have plenty of time. Let's dump these." Grant turned and headed toward the coat check.

Olivia trailed behind him, forcing herself to check out the party, not his very fine ass. If all the chatter and laughter was any indicator, everyone packed into the room was having a tremendous time. Par for the course with the snowboard crew. Especially since tomorrow was a charity exhibition, not a competition.

When they reached the card table with a few rolling coat racks behind it, a pretty brunette smiled and batted her fake eyelashes at Grant. "Well, hi."

Olivia's jaw clenched. Not that she was jealous when his crooked grin appeared in response. But did every single woman who set eyes on Grant have to flirt with him? And since when did she care?

Somehow her arm moved of its own volition and she laid one hand on his shoulder. "Do you want to hold on to the ticket or should I?"

The woman's eyes widened and her lips thinned. Grant was oblivious. He just had "it." Like catnip. Maybe that's why everyone was so attracted to him because they wanted to be the one he noticed.

"Will you hold it in your purse?" Grant handed her the voucher.

She snatched the ticket from him and stuffed it in her silver sequined clutch. She stole a glance at the coat check chick, who pouted and turned to hang up their jackets. Maybe she'd been a little petty. But she and Grant were supposed to be spending time together this weekend, not finding a stranger to kiss at the stroke of midnight.

They turned and surveyed the party. "It's pretty loud in

here. Dance?" Although being pressed close to his lean frame wasn't her most brilliant idea.

Grant rolled his eyes. "Yeah, I'll need another six pack before that's happening. You know I don't dance."

"Hey——you danced with me at prom." She bumped his shoulder.

"Doesn't count. Fifteen years ago. And the three of us went together because we were all single." He snorted. "I saw a hallway leading to what looked like another den or something. Let's check it out."

They wove through the packed room and a few tall Christmas trees sparkling with lights filled the humid air with the scent of fresh pine. It felt more like a Hawaiian luau than a holiday party and Olivia's bangs were sticking to her forehead.

The DJ shouted, "Everyone ready to party?" The crowd roared.

"We're going old school, people!" Prince's "1999" blared through the speakers mounted around the house and everyone started jumping up and down.

Energy surged through her. She loved Prince. "Come on, you can dance to Prince, right?"

"No. I want to sit and catch up with my best girl." Grant caught her hand and tugged her out of the writhing masses.

Maybe he was finally ready to talk to her.

Olivia followed him into what resembled an old-fashioned library and her breath caught in her chest. Floor to ceiling bookshelves stuffed full of leather-bound volumes, complete with mahogany wood sliding ladders formed three of the four walls. The far end of the room was a window framing the mountains, creating the illusion like they were in some enchanted open-air library.

A sprawling cognac-colored leather couch sat before a

broad brick fireplace with an enormous fluffy rug in front of the hearth.

Grant whistled. "Wow. This is your dream room for sure, right?"

She nodded and crossed to one of the shelves, unable to stop herself from stroking the books' spines. "Oh my god, this collection is incredible."

She slid out Oscar Wilde's *The Importance of Being Earnest.* She gazed back at Grant and his eyes gleamed like a lion's. "It is a first edition. Do you have any idea what that's worth? Whose house is this again?"

"I don't have a clue. But I love seeing you so excited." He strode toward her, then pivoted abruptly and sat on the couch.

"Once a bookworm nerd, always a bookworm nerd." Unable to resist, she opened the book, savoring the perfume of old pages and worn leather, one of her favorite smells, ever since she'd discovered the world of reading.

"Well, whoever owns this place must be pretty trusting because this collection is worth a fortune. I better put it back." With a sigh, she carefully shelved the volume. One day, she'd have a library like this.

She turned and another gorgeous vision greeted her. Grant lounged on the sofa, one booted foot crossed over his knee. He raked his long fingers through his thick, messy hair, his eyes closed. In repose, he resembled a subject for a Greek sculpture or painting. She gulped wine, her throat suddenly parched.

His eyes flew open and he patted the cushion next to him, his expression impassive. She strolled toward him, her heart galloping in her chest. *Down, girl.*

Olivia plopped down next to him, mirrored his casual posture, and sipped her wine. "Tell me how your mom is.

She's got to be thrilled you're back at the ranch." There, that was a safe opening.

A smile tugged at his lips. "That's an understatement. For a few months while I was living up in the main house, she cooked every meal for me like when I was a kid."

"Lucky you, she's such an amazing chef. That probably made it tougher to move into the guesthouse."

"Yeah. I go up for dinner most nights. It's nice to be around her and Chris and the rest of the family." Grant took a pull of his longneck beer.

"It's so great that your mom found a second chance at love. And how is it working for your sister Sam?" Okay, she was going to run out of chit-chat soon.

His brows drew together. "Samantha runs the ranch and the breeding operation like clockwork. She's incredible. It's great being outdoors most of the day and the horse breeding season is intense. It works for now, but I've got to figure out what's next."

"Do you feel like you're in limbo? Talk to me, Grant. It's me." She reached out and laid her hand on his muscular thigh and both of them jumped.

Big mistake.

She scooted away and tried to act like connecting with him wasn't setting her system alight. This was getting ridiculous. Damn it. She blew out a breath and braved a glance over at him.

Grant leaned in and cupped her face in his hands, his amber eyes hooded. The blaring music from the party faded away and only the crackling of the fire filled the heavy silence between them. Time stood still while they searched each other's eyes, looking for what, Olivia didn't know.

She couldn't breathe. Couldn't move. Couldn't look away.

Very slowly, he lowered his mouth and brushed his lips against hers, in a whisper-light caress. He was gentle, and her lips parted, welcoming the crisp deliciousness of his breath, the heat from his mouth against hers. Goose bumps erupted from her scalp to her toes.

With a growl, he deepened the kiss, sliding his fingers into her hair and pulling her closer. She moaned and wound her arms around his neck, pressing herself against his sculpted chest. Needing more of him. Heat pooled in her belly and reason flew from her mind.

All that mattered was getting closer. The faint hint of tart lager on his tongue, the scent of his shampoo, his hand stroking down her back, all flamed through her veins.

"Ahem. Hey, excuse me?"

A high-pitched voice broke through and they leapt apart. A wide-eyed girl stood just past the couch's edge with a smirking guy in a rainbow striped sweater and yellow beanie.

Olivia sprang up off the sofa, smoothing her hair back and struggling for composure. *Oh crap.*

"Sorry to interrupt, but are you Grant? The photographer?" The young guy squinted at Olivia for a moment before swinging his gaze to Grant.

To his credit, Grant acted nonchalant, remained seated. "Yeah?"

"Toby sent us to find you. Wants you to meet a couple of the other riders before tomorrow. I can tell him you're busy." His smirk deepened and he waved a scrawny white hand at Olivia.

Olivia's gut clenched. *Double crap.*

Grant stood and narrowed his eyes a fraction. "I'd appreciate it if you didn't. I'll be right there."

The guy held up both hands. "Sure. No problem. They're in the kitchen, in the back of the house."

"C'mon, Rudy." The girl grabbed his arm and they turned and left.

Olivia couldn't meet Grant's eyes. Not only had they kissed, if they hadn't been interrupted, who knew what could have happened? Because the chemistry between them was beyond electric.

"Livvie." Grant's voice was husky.

She inhaled deeply and peered up at him through her lashes. His face was smooth, expressionless, his eyes unreadable in the subdued light of the study. "Grant."

"I don't know what to say." He bit his lip and looked toward the fire. "That was a mistake. I'm sorry."

Heat crept into her cheeks and a hollow feeling settled in her chest. "Wow, this isn't awkward at all." His matter-of-fact dismissal stung. Hell, he'd initiated the kiss.

"Damn it, Livvie, you're my best friend. What the hell. Can you imagine how awkward it would be if that had been Toby? What would we even say?"

Olivia closed her eyes. She was being ridiculous. Of course he was right. But damn it, part of her wanted him to acknowledge the brief kiss had been mind-blowing and toe-curling. At least for her.

"You're right. I know that. He'd be surprised, to say the least." She linked her fingers together and squeezed. Hard enough that her fingernails dug into her palms. She welcomed the bright burst of pain to pull her head out of her ass.

Grant retreated another step. "To say the least. Let's just act like nothing happened. Come on, I need to find Toby."

He turned and strode from the room without another word. Classic Grant.

"I'll meet you in a few. I need a moment." She turned toward the fireplace and stared into the dancing flames. She took a few deep cleansing breaths and glanced at her watch. Crap, it was only ten thirty.

Snapping open her clutch, she fished out her compact and

lip gloss. She reapplied the shiny nude color and considered her appearance. Her cheeks were rosy, partially from heat and partially from lingering embarrassment. Maybe a teeny bit from irritation with Grant's hasty exit.

Grant wasn't the only one with master compartmentalizing skills. Maybe she had led a more sheltered life, but that didn't mean one kiss would ruin the weekend. She'd had to master her game face after her mom's accident and the ensuing years filled with obstacles and disappointment. Toby would never know what had just transpired, at least not from her. And Grant would never suspect how much it had affected her.

She was leaving for Greece in a few months anyway. They'd keep it light for the rest of the weekend and she'd simply make sure not to be alone with him again. They'd just allow things to settle back to normal.

She squared her shoulders and marched out of the study, intent on grabbing another glass of wine and finding her friends. In that order.

CHAPTER 7

Grant stalked through the crowd, silently cursing himself. Shit, damn and double damn. He and Olivia had been sitting on the couch chatting, like they'd done for years. Somehow, he'd lost track of the conversation and fixated on her mouth.

How her lower lip was fuller than her cupid's bow upper lip. How the shiny pink gloss made her straight white teeth even more brilliant, the hint of her pink tongue more tempting. It was like Olivia, his librarian tomboy friend, disappeared and her sexy twin stepped in.

He'd been unable to stop himself from clasping her face, and when her pupils flared and her lips parted, he'd finally captured her lips.

And damn. Kissing her had felt right. A punch of passion to his gut. She'd tasted like earthy red wine, mixed with something uniquely her own. But it was the opposite of right. He could count on one hand the people he trusted to be there through thick and thin. He couldn't afford to lose her, despite wanting to have her come apart in his arms.

"Grant." The shout carried over the pumping bass music.

He glanced up and Toby, with a slender, smiling blonde beside him, was signaling for him to come over.

Grant crisscrossed through the throng. "Hey." He gave a half wave at Toby's crush.

"This is Erin. Erin, this is my best bud, Grant. Where's Olivia?" Toby's brows lifted.

"She should be right behind me." He forced his mind to snap shut.

"Cool. I want you to meet a couple of the riders to spotlight tomorrow. They've been the ringleaders helping me out and they're also the best." Toby waved his arm, gesturing to someone behind him.

Grant glanced back. Two loose-limbed young guys approached them. The tight muscles around his neck softened. Connecting to the snowboard crew would be easy—hanging with the athletes was his comfort zone. Discussing potential shots they wanted to capture tomorrow to obtain some excellent content would give him something to focus on.

The hairs on the back of his neck lifted and he tensed again. The fresh peach-honey aroma of Olivia's hair drifted toward him a moment before she stepped up beside him.

"Hey, guys. You must be Erin." Her wide smile was pasted on and her perfect lips were immaculately glossy once again. "I'm Olivia." She revealed no tension, like nothing had happened in the library.

Erin returned the smile. "Hi, Olivia. Toby's told me so much about you two. Great to meet you. Do you want to head over to the bar with me while these guys talk to Brandon and Jer?"

"Sure. You guys want two more of the same?" Olivia asked, her voice steady and soothing—her librarian voice.

"That'd be great." Grant retreated a step, avoiding brushing against her. He had wanted them to act nonchalant, so why did her cool demeanor feel like a punch in the solar plexus?

The two athletes reached them and he lost himself discussing the highlights of the exhibition, especially hitting the fresh powder by Chair 23 and the Hemlocks. An elbow tapped into his ribs and Erin smiled and offered him a beer.

"Where's Olivia?" Was she avoiding him?

"Oh, we met up with a friend of mine at the bar. They're dancing." Erin smiled and turned to Toby. "You said she's single, right? She is so Jon's type. And he's a good guy."

Toby's lips quirked. "She's amazing, like I told you. Maybe you can introduce Grant to your friend Ashley now."

"No offense, Erin, but I'm not looking to meet anyone." Grant managed not to whip his head around to see who Olivia was with. Barely.

Erin's brow furrowed and she glanced down at her watch. "No worries. But it is New Year's Eve. You don't need a date, but you do need someone to kiss at midnight, which is in around an hour."

Grant closed his eyes for a moment and wished he were anywhere but in the middle of a raging party. He didn't want to kiss anyone other than Olivia, and that wasn't an option.

"There you are. I saw your girlfriend dancing with someone else, so I figured I'd come see if you wanted to dance." The brunette from the coat check appeared at his side and stroked long, fuchsia, coffin-shaped fingernails down his arm.

"That's not his girlfriend, Mandy, she's just a friend," Toby piped in.

Grant gritted his teeth. Sometimes Toby's cheerful openness was a pain in the ass.

"Oh, well in that case, I'm Mandy. Nice to meet you…?" Her dark eyes widened as she caught his hand.

With supreme self-control, he pried off her fingers which

were wrapping around him like tentacles. He stuffed his hand in the pocket of his jeans. It wasn't this girl's fault he was in a mood, but she needed to back off. "Hey, Mandy, I'm Grant."

She giggled and twirled a strand of her long hair. Damn he hated giggling. "Hi, Grant, so how do you know Toby?"

He swallowed his irritation. "We grew up together." He glared at Toby over her head and Toby snickered. The shit-head found his discomfort hilarious.

Maybe she'd just go away if he ignored her. He'd come to Mammoth to hang with his friends and take some killer photos. Do a shoot after six long months. Finally, she started chatting with Erin.

He sipped his beer and scanned the room.

Suddenly, the temperature in the overheated room shot up to boiling. Olivia was plastered against some guy on the dance floor, and the guy had his hands on her ass. Her arms were loosely draped over the guy's massive shoulders. She threw her head back and laughed and swayed to the techno music. She didn't even like techno. The guy stroked one hand up and down her back and Grant's hands balled into fists. What the hell? He growled.

"Dude, what's up with you? You look like you're a bull with a red flag in your face." Toby tugged on his sleeve.

Grant shook him off and started toward the dance floor. "Who the hell's that guy practically dry-humping Olivia? We need to go kick his ass."

Toby grabbed him. "Stop. What's up with you? Erin's friends with him and Olivia can dance with whoever the hell she wants. Looks like she's having a good time to me."

Grant glared down at his friend, who was eyeing him with speculation. He looked back toward Olivia and now she was facing him. She grinned and waved at him and Toby.

Toby elbowed him. "See? She's fine. What's going on?

Mandy's hot, it's New Year's Eve, why don't you have some fun? I know you've had a rough year, but it's time for a fresh start, right? You don't need to hang with Mandy if you're not into her, but don't ruin Livvie's night."

Grant struggled to regulate his racing pulse. Deliberately, he turned back toward Brandon and Jer. He'd keep waxing poetic about powder days and regain control. His ex had accused him on more than one occasion of being able to flip his emotions on and off.

That skill wasn't working where Livvie was concerned right now. Apparently kissing his best friend was turning his world upside down. The one anchor, the one stable force in his life was the Three Musketeers. Without the certainty of their unconditional support, he'd be lost at sea. He would not look at the dance floor again.

But hanging with Mandy or some other random chick wasn't happening. He managed to lose himself in a debate about SnoPlanks versus Burton snowboards and shared a story from the trip where he'd been lucky enough to participate in a shoot in Chamonix, in the South of France. One of the riders, Brandon, was heading to France and Switzerland the following week to ride for the rest of the season. Lucky dude.

The familiar urge to hop on a plane and head somewhere new tore through him with a vengeance. Sure, he'd wanted to, planned to settle down. To make San Diego his home base again, whether he lived at Pacific Vista Ranch or got his own place closer to the beach. But discussing travel stirred his restless streak. The desire to see new places and capture images in fresh ways. The situation with Olivia wasn't helping.

He sensed Olivia's presence before she spoke, felt the heat from her body prior to her greeting them. It was like he had a homing device where she was concerned.

Toby and Erin were off somewhere in the throng, giddy as two teenagers. Mandy had wandered off a while ago, once she'd clued in that he wasn't going to be her hookup for the evening. The guys headed back to find their dates because it was 11:55 p.m.

"You having a good time?" Olivia asked, tilting her head back to look up at him through her thick lashes.

He shrugged. "You sure seem to be." And he sounded like a dick.

She arched a dark brow. "What's that supposed to mean?"

"You seemed pretty cozy with that guy. Where'd he go?"

Olivia's eyes narrowed. "Are you really giving me crap about dancing with someone? You wouldn't dance with me. It is a New Year's Eve party, right? I thought we'd decided to have fun?"

"Sorry. I'm just wiped out. You gonna stay? Because I'm heading back to the condo soon."

She shrugged a shoulder. "No, I'm all partied out. We should check with Toby, although he's going to give us crap for leaving early."

Grant glanced at the window. The snow continued to dump fast and furious, almost obscuring the sky. It would make for excellent powder conditions tomorrow, especially for the boarders who loved to perform tricks. But it would definitely make it tougher to find their way home tonight.

"Probably. But we need him to navigate back to the house in this storm." And they needed Toby so they weren't alone together.

Suddenly, a chant rose over the music. "Ten! Nine! Eight!"

Olivia and Grant's gazes locked. Her bluebell eyes were enormous in her face. It was almost midnight.

Kiss time. And the rest of the party receded and it was just him with Olivia. Alone again with the magnetic pull between them too powerful to resist. Yet, Grant couldn't budge his feet; they were like iron boots nailed to the hard-wood floors.

"Four! Three! Two! One!"

"Oh, damn it." Olivia crossed the small space between them, wound her arms around his neck, and pressed her mouth to his. Grant's paralysis ended when her soft lips and sweet breath touched him. He thrust his hands into her long, silky hair and slanted his mouth across hers, deepening the kiss. Their tongues swirled and stroked and his grip tight-ened on her head, holding her in place while he plundered her mouth.

Cheers erupted around them, dragging him back to the present. He lifted his head and stared into her eyes. Her pupils were huge, the blue irises almost overtaken. Both of them were panting, like they'd just hiked the backside of Mammoth Mountain.

Someone smacked him on the back. "Happy New Year!"

It was a stranger, but suddenly Grant realized how close they'd come to being discovered. It wasn't like Olivia had given him a peck on the lips. They'd been devouring each other in the middle of the throng, oblivious to everyone else. To everything else.

And all he knew was right now, all he wanted was to spirit her back to the condo and spend the beginning of the new year exploring every inch of her perfect little body. All the reasons it was a bad idea didn't seem so important in the moment. He needed to be inside her.

"Grant," she whispered, but he couldn't ignore the matching need in her voice.

Surrendering to impulse, he grabbed her hand and tugged her toward the coat check. She followed without a word. They were on the same page. He didn't want to think past tonight. And all he wanted was Olivia.

They gathered their coats--luckily Mandy wasn't at the coat check--and zigzagged across the room at a healthy trot.

"Happy New Year, guys. Olivia. Grant. Where you going?" Toby stepped into their path and held up a hand. "The night's young."

Olivia squared her shoulders and smiled. "Happy New Year! We were just looking for you. We're heading back to the condo. Neither of us is used to boarding all day and partying all night. Do you and Erin want to come?"

Grant held his breath. If Toby and Erin came, the really bad idea he was about to embark on was going to be shot down in flames. The devil on his shoulder had his fingers crossed that Toby would stay at the party, while the angel on the other side encouraged Toby and Erin to join them.

"Nah. We're going to hang for a while longer." Toby slid his arm around Erin's waist and hugged her in close. "And I'm going to stay at Erin's place tonight."

Grant blew out a breath and Olivia inhaled sharply. They would have the condo to themselves. *Oh shit.*

How were they going to stop this juggernaut now? Short of returning and locking themselves in their respective bedrooms? Because right now, every fiber of his being was ready to throw all reason to the wind and make love to Olivia all night.

Repercussions be damned.

He'd never wanted a woman the way he wanted her and all his reasoning against it had vanished with that last kiss.

When they didn't respond, Toby laughed. "You guys. All you do is go out of the house, turn right and walk seven blocks, turn right again and it's the fifth house on the right. You won't get lost."

Olivia's lips twitched. "I'll make Grant count the houses. It's a monster blizzard out there. You aren't driving, right?"

Erin shook her head. "I'm right across the street, so we're set."

"Just don't forget to meet up at the top of the gondola at seven forty five to get some pre-expo shots, okay?" Toby said.

Grant nodded. "No problem. I'll probably crash as soon as we get back to our place." *Liar.* He couldn't go to sleep right now if his life depended on it. Not with Olivia in the house with him. Not tonight.

They said their good-byes and wove through the crowd to the front door. They paused to bundle up. Livvie pulled on her hot-pink beanie with a giant pom-pom low on her forehead and stuffed her small hands into patterned mittens. She looked adorable with her coat zipped to her chin. He almost grabbed her and kissed the tip of her small nose but fished out his own gloves instead.

Warmth filled his chest and a sense of happiness permeated his being. A feeling he hadn't had in longer than he could recall. Being with Olivia had always made him content. They knew each other so well and were so comfortable in every situation. Even with his nerves thrumming, and the potential disaster of what he was contemplating doing with her tonight, the warmth remained.

The door flew open and along with a group of revelers, what felt like a bucket full of snow blew into their faces. Olivia squealed and jumped back.

"We're off to an auspicious start to our walk home. My god, this is like something out of a movie. I've never seen such a snowstorm." Livvie peered out. "You think we'll find the house?"

Grant nodded. "I've got us covered." He reached for her and tucked her arm into the crook of his elbow. "Just hold on tight."

She shifted closer to him and gripped his forearm. "Let's do this."

Together, they stumbled out into the blizzard and trudged up the street. They kept their heads lowered against the bitter wind slapping their cheeks. He looked up and caught the street sign where they needed to turn. Thank god he'd paid attention.

"Fifth house on the right. We can do this." His foot slipped and he couldn't control his descent, falling on his ass and dragging Olivia down with him. They landed in a heap on the ice-skating rink excuse for a sidewalk.

For a minute they lay there laughing, their breath distinct, visible puffs in the air. But what had to be sub-zero windchill temperatures sliced right through their jackets and Grant shivered. "Sorry. Come on, we've got to get inside." He stood and pulled Olivia to her feet.

Under the rays of light streaming down from the street-lamp, the snowflakes danced around them. "Turn around and I'll brush you off and you get me. Otherwise, we'll be soaked."

Grant turned and Olivia stroked and patted his back. Even through all the layers of his coat and sweater, heat flamed simply from her hands on him. Insane. He whirled around and grabbed her hand. "Come on. Let's go."

No way could he start touching her right now. He would never be able to stop. And some unlucky neighbor would stumble upon two frostbitten bodies. They hurried, though it was like slogging through quicksand.

"Hey, I'm still covered with snow." She strode along next to him.

"We're almost there. Hold on. We'll be in the Jacuzzi in ten minutes."

"There it is." Olivia pointed at the redwood A-frame that sparkled with lights under the full moon. They trekked up the hill and climbed the snow-covered stairs.

Grant opened the door and they fell inside and slammed the door, closing away the blizzard behind them.

"Fire or Jacuzzi first?" Grant whipped off his hat and unzipped his down jacket.

Livvie had already tossed her hat onto the granite countertop and was shaking the snow from her thick wavy hair. "Jacuzzi. I'll run up and grab my suit. Is any wine open?"

"I'm going to pop the champagne. Meet you outside in five."

She hurried off up the stairs and Grant scrubbed his hands along his jaw. Okay. Maybe they'd just hang out in the Jacuzzi like friends and have fun. The icy weather had definitely sobered him up and perhaps a little bit of reason was creeping back into his addled brain.

He grabbed the champagne bottle and two plastic flutes. He could do this. She was his best friend. They'd just been caught up in the holiday madness. That was all. It was an urge and their relationship was worth more than a hookup that could damage it forever. Determined, he opened the bottle and set it down on the counter.

He'd get on his swim trunks and meet her in the Jacuzzi. They'd have some laughs and bubbly and then go to sleep. Separately. No problem.

"I thought you'd be in the hot tub by now. Go change and I'll take out the drinks."

Grant glanced up and every inch of him leapt to attention. Her hair was up in one of those messy topknots again, with a few tendrils around her flushed cheeks. Her bikini was fire-engine red and showed off just how all that surfing and athletic activity gave her the taut physique with curves in all the right places. He gulped.

He was in hot water, and not the simmering bubbles awaiting them in the Jacuzzi.

CHAPTER 8

"Hello, earth to Grant. I'm getting in because it is freezing, so come on." Olivia's voice was husky, and she couldn't meet his eyes when she snatched up the bottle and glasses.

He was staring at her like he'd just been struck over the head by a board, flummoxed. She smiled to herself--she was confident in her bikini and comfortable in her skin. Her body was strong because she loved exercising outdoors and the endorphins calmed her overactive brain. If all the activity resulted in nice abs, she'd take them as the side benefit.

Without looking back to see if his jaw was still on the floor, she opened the French doors to the covered deck and the glacial wind slammed into her like a wall of cement. Quickly, she set down the bottle and glasses and whipped open the hot tub lid, gratefully inhaling the steam rising from the water. She flipped on the switch and the jets roared to life.

She poured the champagne into the glasses, set the bottle and Grant's drink on the adjacent table, and climbed the two wide steps to slide into the Jacuzzi. She hissed out a breath when the almost boiling water seared into her skin. The contrast with the freezing cold air was striking and seductive. Kind of like the contrast between viewing Grant as her best friend for the last almost twenty years and suddenly wanting nothing more than to kiss him forever.

They'd crossed a line and there was no going back.

Not after that kiss.

Not after that smug feeling inside from watching him seethe with jealousy when she was dancing with another guy.

Not after witnessing the emotion in his eyes. She knew him too well. Where others would always marvel at how impassive and cool he'd act, kind of like a modern-day Clint Eastwood, she generally had him figured out. In a way only possible in a relationship that dated back to grade school.

Now fate had stepped in and they were alone tonight. They were both single. Their chemistry was explosive. Maybe her new life of adventure started tonight, not in a few months when she flew to Greece.

Even if things became awkward between them, a little space would allow that to dissipate in no time. Their friendship had endured decades and there was no reason they couldn't get this out of their systems tonight. Tomorrow would be hectic with the competition, then they'd head home, and back to their busy lives.

Because she was so hot for him right now, she didn't think she could resist and couldn't come up with a single reason why she should. And if she was correct, he was on the same page. Same line even. She'd use every single analytical tool in her librarian brain to rationalize it.

It would be fine. Rationalization complete.

Grant jogged out, grabbed his glass, and joined her in the steamy water. Even though he slid in up to his shoulders, she hadn't missed the way his lean, square pecs had a sprinkling of dark hair that narrowed into a trail down his sculpted abs before disappearing into his turquoise board shorts. Steam wafted up around him and he sucked in a breath.

"Damn, this reminds me of when I went to Iceland and we were in these outdoor natural hot springs called The Blue Lagoon. Pretty extreme. Brrr." He sank in up to his chin, holding his glass aloft. Beads of moisture danced along his carved-from-marble arm.

His reaction made her snicker. "You're so dramatic. But you're right. I'm so used to San Diego weather, I don't know what I'd do if I had to contend with these conditions regularly. I like it seventy and sunny."

"Spoiled. But absolutely correct. Hold this." He shoved his glass into her hand, their fingers brushing and sparking every nerve ending in her system. He dunked his head beneath the surface and rose, smoothing his hair back. "Okay, that helped."

She returned his glass and toasted with hers. "Happy New Year."

"Happy New Year." His lips quirked up. "So."

She drew in a deep breath. "So. What should we do?" She wanted more of him. She wasn't changing her mind. Was he going to make her ask?

His golden eyes hooded and his smile grew wicked. "I've got a few ideas."

For a moment, neither of them moved. Olivia's skin heated, and not simply from the Jacuzzi's extreme temperature. Carpe diem.

Now or never. She crooked a finger, beckoning him closer.

Even in the shadowed light, Olivia couldn't miss the flare of his pupils. Without breaking her gaze, Grant scooted along the hard seat until their shoulders touched. Olivia angled herself on the seat to face him, taking another sip of champagne as anticipation danced along her skin. She was trembling, her heart galloping in her chest.

"Finish it." Grant nodded toward her drink and then swallowed his in one gulp. He took her plastic glass and tossed them both over the edge.

He pounced, his hands spanning her waist, picking her up, and placing her on his lap. She adjusted her legs and wiggled in a little closer, so the ridge of his rock-hard arousal dug into her center. Tingles shot up her spine and she groaned, her head dropping back, her lips parting. She slid her hands up his slick, toned pecs and looped her arms around his neck.

He tugged her closer and her breasts crushed against him, the bare skin of their torsos slick and hot. He growled and kissed the hollow of her throat, trailing his lips up her neck, to the sensitive spot beneath her ear. Chills erupted on her skin and her nipples leapt to attention. One hand slipped into her hair and the other tugged the skimpy material aside until she was bare to him. His lips descended, and he raked his teeth back and forth across her taut nipple before capturing it in his mouth.

Sensation shot through her, her back bowed, and she dug her fingers into his damp hair. "More." She moaned and held his head in place.

"You like that. What else do you like?" He murmured against her skin as he shifted his attention to her other breast. He stroked one hand down her spine to the top of her ass and teased his fingertips along the edge of her bikini bottom.

Oh god, he was a talker and wasn't that her favorite? She shivered and melted closer to him.

"You're doing good so far." She dragged his head up and slanted her mouth across his. Her skin flamed and little shivers wracked her body as his tongue stroked and danced with hers.

He paused for a moment, leaning back to gaze into her eyes. "You cold?" His jaw was tight, his eyes warm honey.

She leaned in until the tips of their noses touched. "Not even a little bit."

"You're trembling." The crisp flavor of champagne lingered on his breath, along with a tart flavor that was all his own.

"I'm excited." She rocked her hips, savoring his sharp intake of breath. "Can't you tell?"

His hands tightened on her hips and then he stroked calloused palms up her back, imprinting her against him. "I'm excited too. Can you tell?" He arched one dark brow.

He captured her mouth and one hand descended and slipped into the front of her bathing suit bottom. He cupped her and explored her with long, blunt fingers. She jolted and bit his lower lip. He shifted so her clit pressed into the heel of his hand, then slid one finger inside her. Then two.

They groaned simultaneously. His talented fingers went to work and she rode his hand, on the brink of exploding. Helpless to slow down the sensations slamming through her system.

"You feel so damn good." He gritted the words out without breaking their kiss.

"Mmm…I'm so close. Don't stop." She deepened the kiss to keep from screaming. Waves of sensation rose within her and she bucked against him until she came apart.

She moaned and her head dropped onto his shoulder, her entire body going limp and heavy on top of him. She pressed her lips onto the slick skin of his broad shoulder, savoring the salty taste of his skin. Her mind was blissfully blank and she couldn't tell where her body ended and his began.

Grant stroked his hands up and down her back, his

caresses leaving a trail of fire along her spine. "Happy New Year." He murmured against her hair.

Her lips curved and she shifted back. "I'd say it's started out quite well. Let me make yours as good as mine." She snaked her hand down his stomach and made quick work of the ties straining to hold the top of his shorts together.

He dropped his head back on the ledge and groaned. "Olivia."

She grasped his hefty erection in her hand, marveling how her fingers couldn't quite wrap all the way around him. His skin was smooth and silky here, his cock pure steel. She stroked him from base to tip, relishing the sharp staccato puffs of air floating into the icy evening night.

"Is this okay? Tell me what you want." She whispered the words. Wanting to please him as easily as he'd pleased her.

"I want to be inside you. Right now." The words rumbled in his chest.

Her fingers clenched on him harder, her insides completely molten. Ready. But...

"What about protection?"

He lifted his head and stared into her eyes. "I've tested clean and it's been almost a year. What about you?"

Her eyes widened. "A year? Um, well, me too. And I'm on the pill." She'd been on the pill since she was seventeen when debilitating periods had made her miss school one too many times.

He reached one hand down and tore her bottoms off, leaving them to float around or who knew where they went. Who cared? He slid his hand along her inner thigh and took two fingers, then three inside her.

She gasped. The feeling of fullness was exquisite. She ached to take all of him inside her. He'd probably split her in half and right now, she was fine with that.

They shifted around, the water sloshing over the rim of

the hot tub. She gripped his shoulders and he brought his hands back to her hips, moving her until she was straddling him. Inch by sweet inch, she sank down until all she could feel was his hot, hard length inside her. Her breath whooshed out.

"Stay right there a minute." His teeth were gritted, his voice raspy, his fingers digging into her ass, holding her immobile. "You feel incredible."

She moaned at the feeling of being impaled on him, the pressure so tight and delicious. Almost overwhelming. But she was greedy for more. She kissed him and slid her fingers into his damp hair, scratching her short nails along his scalp, savoring his harsh breathing.

She began rocking front and back and then experimentally rose up and slid back down. Her muscles clenched and gripped around him--her legs started to shake.

"Oh yeah." He groaned and one hand slid up to clasp her breast. He pinched and rolled her nipple, shooting direct sparks to her flaming center. "Ride me, take what you want."

She found the perfect pressure right where she needed it. Every stroke was liquid fire. Delicious. Pushing her to her limits. Her head dropped back and the cry rose in her throat. Wave after wave of pleasure swept through her. He murmured her name against her skin.

Once she'd stilled, his hands gripped her hips again and started thrusting upward, every stroke branding her with his need. He stroked faster, harder until he came with a roar.

Their harsh, hot breath filled the chilly air. Slowly, other sensations besides Grant's lean frame beneath her began to filter into her awareness. The icy wind blowing against her bare back, the creaking of branches weighed down by heavy snow, the silence of the mountain night.

She shifted back, suddenly shy. They stared at each other for a moment and then Grant reached up and smoothed the loose strands of hair stuck to her face back from her cheeks. "Hi."

"Hi yourself." Grant's smile had a hint of shyness too. "Why don't we get inside and clean up. I'm thirsty."

Yes, that's what they would do. Go inside. What would their impulsive decision look like under the lights?

CHAPTER 9

They scrambled out of the hot tub. Grant grabbed the champagne and they tumbled into the blessedly warm house, slick and slippery and satisfied. As she slammed the door behind her, Olivia's legs wobbled, her mind blurry from the champagne. Or maybe from the earth-shattering orgasms?

She had come apart in her best friend's arms. Shared the most passionate, explosive sex she'd ever had. Sure, she'd figured it would be great, based on their newfound attraction. But she hadn't expected it to be life changing.

She peeked at Grant and her breath lodged in her throat. He lounged against the sofa's edge, his skin gleaming in the firelight, bronzed and hard and beautiful. "So maybe we should talk about this?" He gestured between them, his voice husky.

She glanced down at her wet, naked body and a wave of *something* flowed through her. While she was confident in a bikini, standing naked in the fully lit condo was out of her comfort zone. Clothes. She needed clothes.

"I'm freezing. I'm going to grab some sweats first." She

hightailed it across the room and up the stairs, his topaz eyes burning holes through her back. Cowardly, maybe. But she needed a minute to regain her composure.

She grabbed a towel from the ensuite bathroom and dried off the remaining droplets of water from her overheated skin. Her reflection in the mirror revealed her sexy smoky eye had morphed into more of a raccoon mask. Between the snow, steam, and sex, she looked thoroughly disheveled, but satisfied.

After washing her face and smoothing on some moisturizer, Olivia slid into her comfy charcoal fleece sweats and favorite faded yellow "Librarians Rule" hoodie. She brushed out her bedhead hair and bundled it up into a top knot again. Now she looked more like the Olivia that Grant was accustomed to, so would they slip back into their friendship roles when she descended the stairs?

He wanted to talk, so she'd propose they make the most of their one night together. They'd already crossed the point of no return, but she'd gauge Grant's reaction. Maintaining their friendship was her number one priority. But her pulse kicked up, picturing them making love on the fluffy rug in front of the fireplace.

She returned to the main room and Grant stood at the kitchen island shoveling in a piece of pizza. He wore his gray sweats low on his hips, emphasizing the perfect Vs of muscle leading down...there. His hair was slicked back from his square-jawed face and his sculpted chest was bare.

Damn, she'd seen him without a shirt hundreds of times, but now it was through an entirely different lens. The "hot guy I want to jump your bones" lens. She sucked in a deep breath––because that body of his tempted her to swoop.

"Did you save me a slice?" Her voice came out a little shaky.

He nodded and swept one arm toward the counter. "I poured you some ice water. Figured you're dehydrated too."

Swallowing the hint of uncertainty rising in her chest, she crossed the room and grabbed the glass without meeting his eyes. Maybe some cool water would help settle her nerves before their discussion.

"Doing it" versus "talking about doing it" were two very different things.

"Thanks, I definitely needed that." She bit into the generous slice.

He stepped closer, the warmth from his skin palpable. "Aren't you going to look at me?"

She met his gaze, dropped the pizza onto the plate, and licked her lips. "Grant."

He reached for her hands, intertwining their fingers. "So, I think we should agree tonight is just for us. Our secret. We'll go back to the friend zone tomorrow."

Sparks danced up her arms from warmth of his strong hands. "Yes, and we need to promise each other that sex won't mess up our friendship."

His brows drew together, his gaze searching hers. "Yeah, sex won't mess up our friendship. You won't lose me. Or us."

Her belly clenched and she nibbled on her lower lip. "And Toby. He can't suspect anything--especially when we made such a big deal about him talking about hookups."

"Tomorrow we are back to the Three Musketeers." He gripped her hands tighter.

She inhaled a calming breath and nodded. She pushed away the flash of uncertainty. She could handle it.

His gaze dropped to her lips and he growled. "Olivia."

He tugged her against his broad hard chest. His mouth slanted across hers and his long fingers dug into her hair. He deepened the kiss and she inhaled his delicious taste, savored the stroke of his tongue against hers, basked in his powerful embrace. Reservations evaporated and sensation took over. She wound her arms around his neck and abandoned herself to the myriad of sensations pulsing through her.

His clean scent surrounded her and every nerve ending tingled and burned. Without breaking their kiss, he swept her up in his arms and carried her toward the roaring fire. He gently lowered them to the sheepskin rug, settling his weight between her spread legs.

He sat back on his knees and tugged her sweatshirt off, tossing it across the room. He leaned down and his gaze swept along her bare torso. She shivered under his perusal, her nipples tightening, her center melting.

"You are the most beautiful woman I've ever seen." His eyes hooded and he descended, his lips brushing along her collarbone, traveling to one shoulder and across to the other, leaving a trail of goose bumps. Her back arched up to meet him.

His mouth traveled across her skin and captured one breast, teasing and biting her aching nipples. Desire surged through her, quick and intense. "Every inch of you is perfect."

He continued down her body, licking and scraping his teeth lightly along her hipbones, setting her to trembling and moaning again. Her hips bucked and he reached down with one hand and slowly dragged her sweats down, following the path with his sensual kisses.

Olivia dug her hands into his hair and rocked her hips against him. His mouth was wicked, talented, hot. And she couldn't get enough. His powerful hands clasped her hips, lifting her and sliding her pants all the way off. He knelt between her legs, pressed featherlight kisses up her thigh, nuzzling the tender skin, and switched his attention to her other leg, teasing her.

"Grant." If he didn't kiss her where she needed him right now, she'd die.

"I'm going to take good care of you, sweetness." He murmured against her skin before finally, finally licking her in one long stroke.

She bowed up, but he held her still, and spread her apart. Circling his tongue along her sensitive bud, tasting her, savoring her like she was the most delicious treat he'd ever had. She moaned as the pleasure surged up in her faster than she could control.

He thrust one blunt finger inside her, added another, and tremors pulsated through her until she cried his name as she came.

He never stopped until she'd settled. He slowly kissed his way up her body, her skin erupting in goose bumps wherever he touched. When he captured her mouth once again, she tasted herself on his lips. Their skin was slick, beaded with perspiration. She stroked her hands up his muscular back, her fingernails digging into his firm shoulders. He lifted his head and gazed into her eyes, his gleaming with desire and question.

"Yes. Now." She ached to have him inside her.

He groaned and slid home in one stroke. He filled her to bursting, her body welcoming his thick, solid length. She wrapped her legs around his waist and pulled him closer, deeper. They found their rhythm, smooth and unhurried, as if they'd done this countless times before. He gripped her ass and tilted her up to meet him and the intensity of their connection rippled through her. When he caught a tender spot her neck in a love bite, she gripped him tighter, urged him on. They moved faster, harder, deeper until the climax built and she burst in a myriad of starlight and he cried her name and fell over the edge with her.

～

GRANT NUZZLED against Livvie's satiny skin, inhaling her sweet scent. He wasn't sure he could move, but he didn't want to crush her and rolled to his side, pulling her with him so they were pressed nose to nose.

"Hi," she whispered, her big blue eyes heavy-lidded, her jaw soft.

"Hi yourself." He swept her thick bangs back from her forehead, her dark hair a wild halo around her face.

"So, that was amazing." Her kiss-plumped lips curved upward.

His lips quirked and he cupped her face in one hand. "You're amazing."

A comfortable silence fell between them, a familiar quiet they'd always shared. For most of their lives, they'd sought comfort from each other. Despite the two wild sex sessions tonight, the feeling remained.

"You are." She pressed a light kiss on his lips, playful now.

He gathered her closer, sliding one leg between her slender, strong ones, stroking his hands up her sleek back. "Let's go to bed––will you brave sleeping with the snorer?"

She giggled. "I guess I'll give you a chance."

He rose, drawing her to her feet. "My room's closer. And you wore me out, woman."

He flipped off the indoor lights, and holding hands, led her into his bedroom, confident the fire would burn itself out in a few hours. He glanced up at the clock and cursed under his breath.

"What's wrong?"

"It's almost three a.m. I'll be lucky if I'll be able to see out of my camera lens tomorrow." He was too old to be up this late, but damn, was every minvute worth it.

"Oh wow, that is late. Let me clean up and I'll be right back." Olivia headed to the bathroom.

Grant scanned the room and tossed the ski gear he'd

dumped on the bed into a pile on the floor. Olivia was obsessively tidy and he was the polar opposite. The clothes were out of the way now, which would have to be good enough. He turned on the small bedside lamp and closed the blinds, shrouding the room in semidarkness.

Olivia returned just as he yanked the chocolate suede comforter to the foot of the bed, revealing smooth, toast-colored sheets. "That bed looks like heaven."

He sat down on the sheets and patted the bed beside him. "Come here."

Her sweatshirt skimmed the tops of her thighs. She looked tousled and sexy and sweet as she crossed the room to him. She perched on the edge of the bed, tilted her head, her white teeth catching her plump lower lip.

When she didn't budge, he reached for her, nestled her into his arms, and dragged the bedspread over them. She softened and snuggled against him, the curve of her cheek pressing against his chest. He dropped a kiss on the top of her dark head, inhaling her honey-peach scent. For tonight, she was his.

"So, Happy New Year." She shifted her head onto the crook of his shoulder and her eyes met his in the subdued light.

He smiled. "Best New Year's Eve celebration I've ever had." Something tightened in his chest. Those weren't just words, they were the truest words he'd uttered in years.

Her lips curved upward. "Me too. I still can't believe I'm here with you like this." She shook her head slightly, her expression bemused.

His arms banded around her, tightening of their own volition. "Yeah. It's a little surreal, but..." *it feels exactly right. Natural.*

Livvie's eyes narrowed, questioning as she examined his face. She reached up one slender finger and stroked it along his cheekbone, then brushed her thumb against his lower lip. His skin heated beneath her touch.

"But somehow it feels just right." Her hand continued its path tracing down to where his pulse thrummed in the hollow of his throat. "We agreed this was just going to be one night, get it out of our systems, and go back to normal, right?"

He forced a half-smile, but a weight settled around his heart. "Yeah, you're right. What happens in Mammoth, stays in Mammoth."

"Well, we still have a few hours and I for one would like to spoon and go to sleep." She turned and shifted back into his arms.

She wiggled in closer, her heart-shaped ass pushing into his burgeoning erection. Holy hell, he hadn't wanted a woman this way in a long time, if ever.

He slid one hand down her toned stomach and cupped her. He nuzzled her neck and whispered in her ear, "I'm suddenly awake again. How about we make tonight last a little longer?"

She arched her spine and rocked her hips into his hand. "Sleep is overrated."

Plenty of time for regrets tomorrow.

CHAPTER 10

Olivia shook her head, groggy from lack of sleep, and attempted to identify the incessant buzzing sound yanking her from her lovely dreamless slumber. Had a mosquito survived the snowstorm and invaded her bedroom? When the insistent noise persisted, she reached up to swat it--anything to shut it up--and encountered a wall of firm muscle instead.

Her eyes flew open, and she blinked furiously to knock the cobwebs from her brain. Grant was sprawled on his belly next to her, his head buried under a pillow, and he hadn't budged. The buzzing had stopped, thank god, but she had a bigger problem on her hands.

Warmth flooded her cheeks as her gaze drifted down Grant's long, sinewy frame. The sheets covered him up to his waist, his beautifully sculpted back and shoulders tempting her to stroke her fingertips along his spine.

In the heat of passion last night, it had all seemed like a simple plan, one they could both handle. They'd loved each other forever. Had each other's backs forever. Trusted each other--and there were probably only a handful of people that either of them truly trusted. And now they had a secret.

In the pale morning light filtering down from the enormous skylight above the bed, he resembled one of Michelangelo's masterpieces. A soft snore was the only sound in the room and affirmed that this was no marble statue next to her, but a living breathing soul.

And who ever thought it was a good idea to have skylights in bedrooms needed to have their head examined––bedrooms were for sleeping and should be fully shrouded in darkness.

The heat in her cheeks flared again. Well, a bedroom should be dark for the sleeping portion anyway. Not that they'd gotten much sleep. They both knew the night was a magical escape and everything went back to friendship in the morning. Kind of like when Cinderella's carriage went full pumpkin at midnight.

Grant looked younger in sleep, the grooves along his mouth softened. The last few years had left a mark on him, but of course since he was a man, the crinkles fanning out from his eyes and lines merely made him look more handsome. She studied him, the artistic side of her appreciating the lines and angles and sheer male beauty. The woman in her wanted him again, but their one dreamy night was over.

She'd simply have to store last night into her memory bank, only to be taken out for herself, probably while she was in the shower alone.

One amber eye cracked open and then widened comically as his lips parted. "Livvie." His voice was gravelly with sleep.

Before she could reply, the buzzing resumed. "God, what is that?" Now that she'd confirmed it was indeed not a mosquito.

Grant rolled and stumbled off the bed toward a heap of clothes across the room. "My phone. Crap, what time is it?"

Olivia had no clue. The cloudy, opaque sky was light but offered no indication if the sun had risen.

He pawed through the garments, tossing them over his shoulder. "Found it." He seized the phone and glanced at the screen.

"It's six-thirty and it's Toby." He held up one finger in front of his mouth.

Olivia didn't need prompting to stay silent. She located her sweatshirt, which lay strewn across the nightstand. She snatched it up and pulled it over her head. As if Toby could see that she was in Grant's bed. Thank god it wasn't a video call.

Nonetheless, the layer of fabric provided a shield between her and Grant's naked glory. His lack of self-consciousness was playing havoc with her imagination. It was only an hour ago she'd been wrapped up in those sinewy arms, with her hands on that very fine ass. Their agreement was one night.

Only one night.

One secret night, to be forever locked away. Today was about supporting Toby and his charity event. For best friends. For the Three Musketeers.

"Sorry man, I was asleep. Wait, what?" He shoved his fingers through his thick hair and glanced over his shoulder at her. His dark brows drew together.

"Hold on, let me go out to the living room so I can see what's up." His usually smooth baritone crackled with annoyance.

Grant stalked out of the room, naked with raging morning wood. Was he trying to kill her or was he just that oblivious of his masculine beauty? He'd never been much of a morning person. Did he just hang around the house naked all the time?

And why did that idea cause her heartrate to skyrocket?

She'd get him some clothes, pronto, because she also

needed to know what was going on. Ignoring the tornado he'd created, she spotted his gray sweats and grabbed them before following Tarzan into the living room.

He'd grabbed the fluffy, kelly green throw from the couch and wrapped it around him. He stood in front of the enormous French doors gazing outside, rubbing his jaw with one hand.

It took a minute for Olivia to focus on the vision through the broad expanse of glass. White. White sky. White snow. White drifts of snow on the balcony railings. The only visible contrast was the scene of the crime, the Jacuzzi.

Not that she'd ever been a fan of what some people found to be an exciting layer of challenge, but the last whiteout she'd experienced had redirected the trajectory of her life. She'd planned on observing the games with Toby today, but right now that looked like a no. Full stop.

No way would she venture onto the slopes in these conditions.

Poor Grant wouldn't have an easy time capturing great shots in this type of environment.

"Man, I'm so sorry. This blows. But I get it. Yeah, I'll tell Livvie." He paused and listened. "Tomorrow? Seriously? You're not coming back at all?"

Grant laughed. "Got it. I guess that's a silver lining. You think you'll be able to dig out and the roads will be cleared by the morning then? All right, we'll be here."

Olivia stiffened as the one-sided conversation sank in. The roads weren't plowed?

First things first. She tossed him his sweats. He needed to cover up so they could switch back to friend mode before Toby returned.

Grant turned and caught the pants, the blanket pooling around his ankles. She quickly averted her eyes and ignored the frisson of excitement shooting up her spine.

No more temptation.

"Looks like it never stopped snowing. What did Toby say?" Time to focus on logistics.

He stalked to the kitchen area and wrenched open a cabinet before answering. "Coffee. Let's make some coffee and I'll fill you in."

She joined him and grabbed the jar of ground French Roast. "I'll make it. Your version tastes like tar. Tell me what's going on."

He huffed and sat on one of the stools at the island, irritation radiating off him. "Mountain is closed. There was an avalanche last night--"

Her breath hitched. She carefully placed the jar onto the counter and turned to him. "Was anyone hurt?"

His expression softened, his eyes warming to honey. "No. Oh Livvie, I'm sorry I should have told you that first. Nobody was hurt."

She exhaled a shaky breath. "It's been years, but those words get me every time. So nobody was hurt?" She gestured with one hand for him to continue.

Grant crossed the room and pulled her into a hug. She snuggled against his bare chest. It was familiar yet no longer familiar. Despite countless shared hugs, now she had a new awareness of him that hadn't existed before last night.

"The avalanche was over on the back side. But the snow isn't supposed to stop until this afternoon and it is whiteout conditions everywhere. The mountain won't open any of the runs--too risky. The event is canceled and Toby's staying at Erin's today." He kept her cocooned in his embrace, his chin resting on the top of her head.

"Poor Toby. All the planning and the charity and all of it. What a waste." She ignored the weakness in her knees and her urge to kiss his smooth skin.

Grant stepped back and grasped her shoulders, creating

some space between them. "I wouldn't call last night a waste." He winked and his crooked grin lit up his face.

Olivia laughed, just like he'd meant her to. He always knew how to cheer her up. "Definitely not a word I'd use. But…"

"Caffeine. Please. I'll be right back." He released her and crossed toward his room.

Olivia gripped the counter and struggled to regulate her breathing. If Grant noticed she was practically hyperventilating, she could always blame it on the altitude, right? She stretched her arms overhead and exhaled a wavering breath.

Coffee. She'd make coffee and breakfast. She pulled out eggs, sharp cheddar, spinach, tomatoes, and asparagus to whip up omelets to go with the croissants they'd picked up at the market. She was ravenous.

Probably all the nocturnal activities. She pressed her hands to her cheeks, the heat rising again at the flashes of sensual memories––the contrast of silky tanned skin beneath her fingertips to the tough sinew of his leanly muscled frame. His clean, slightly salty masculine scent filling her senses. The taste of his sweet warm breath. The perfect fullness of him inside her.

The natural rhythm they'd found effortlessly, as if their emotional connection had paved the way for them to be in sync in bed too. No matter what they said about everything going back to friendship today, nerves fluttered in her belly because everything was different.

It would have been one thing if they were spending the day on the mountain with Grant shooting pictures and her hanging with Toby. They'd have had a natural separation. A cooling off period. But now apparently, they wouldn't see Toby again until tomorrow and they were snowed in for the next twenty-four hours.

Alone together.

Without distractions.

The coffee pot dinged and Grant appeared. She hadn't even heard him approach.

"You still take almond milk, right?" he asked while pouring the steaming black brew into the yellow coffee cups she'd set on the counter.

"Yep. Veggie omelets still your favorite?" *Focus on breakfast for now.* She busied her hands with the food.

Grant set down her mug and wrapped one muscular arm around her from behind. Grant's breath tickled her ear. "Yeah."

The hairs on the back of her neck lifted, and tingles sparked down her spine. She stepped aside, out of his tempting embrace.

"Hey. We have a deal, remember? Back to best friends today." Unable to meet his eyes, she sipped her coffee. Now her system was aflame from his proximity. He wasn't playing fair.

"Livvie." His voice was husky. "Look at me."

She peered up at him through her thick bangs and once again, her breath caught in her throat. He looked serious now; all hints of playfulness had vanished.

His eyes hooded. "It's just you and me until tomorrow. I think we should renegotiate."

"Renegotiate?" Her lips parted.

"The way I see it, we've got plenty of time to be best friends again tomorrow when we head home." He shrugged one bare shoulder. "I mean, why not make the most of today?"

"Make the most of?" Her pulse thrummed in her temples.

He grinned, set down his cup, and turned her to face him. His hands stroked up and down her arms, sparking flickers of electricity. "Yes, little parrot. Make the most of. Last night was incredible. Let's extend our original deal until the morning?"

The heat in Olivia's cheeks promptly shot straight down, pooling in her belly. One night had been more potent than she could have ever dreamed, but another twenty-four hours alone together? Her emotions were already careening around like a pinball ricocheting against immovable objects after one night of shared intimacy. Would she be able to handle more?

Olivia retreated and crossed over to the French doors, contemplating the blizzard outside. They were in a cocoon. A bubble. The only two people who would know how they'd spent their time snowed in together would be her and Grant.

And weren't they the only two that mattered? She didn't really care what anyone else thought, besides Toby. But....

But for decades she and Grant had been each other's safe harbor and you could only rock that boat so much before it capsized forever. If she actually fell for her best friend, would they be able to step back and return to their friendship? Could she pretend to love him platonically if she actually fell in love?

Because their lovemaking had been beyond anything she'd ever experienced before. And that made it dangerous.

"Livvie?" Grant's voice echoed the sliver of doubt that permeated her being.

She turned and forced herself to meet his clear gaze. The doubt was being trounced by the desire coursing through her. "I'm scared."

His brow furrowed. "Livvie--"

"I need more caffeine. Let's sit down and talk about this." She returned to the kitchen and grabbed her mug. Gazed down to see the mug's ironic slogan: *Love the one you're with.*

He followed her to the couch and sat on the opposite end. Maintaining some distance. She curled her legs beneath her and waited. When he didn't say anything, she dove in.

"Look, last night was incredible." The burning in her cheeks just wouldn't quit. "And part of that was our inhibitions were lowered. We'd been drinking. It was safe to look at it as one secret night. But if we keep going today…"

"It wasn't because we were drinking." He shook his head. "But I hear you. And if you really want to step back right now, I respect that. I guess I just feel happier than I have in a long time and that's because of you."

"Because of the sex or because you're hanging with your best friend?" She laughed--this was her Grant, and their lifelong ability to laugh together remained unchanged. The combination of attraction and amusement felt good.

His lips twitched. "All of it. I mean, you're pretty amazing in every way."

Her heart walloped against her ribs. "You too." Hadn't she always thought he'd make some woman deliriously happy one day?

He carefully set down his mug on the low wooden coffee table and scooted a few inches closer. "We'll have to keep this secret anyway, right?" The shallow dimples in his lean cheeks deepened.

"Keeping the secret isn't what I'm worried about." She nibbled on the inside of her cheek. "I can't lose you as a friend. Can you promise we'll be able to sort this out?"

"Look, Livvie, my life is a mess right now, I can't guarantee anything. But nothing would ever be able to ruin our friendship." His words were confident, but his tone wasn't quite as forceful as she would have preferred.

She squeezed her eyes closed and drew in a deep breath. Damn it, nothing was guaranteed--she'd learned that lesson several years ago. Life could change on a whim and if happiness was within reach, you grabbed it with both hands. Grant made her happy, even if part of that happiness was the mind-blowing sex. And she was leaving for Greece in two months, the first step to reclaiming her lost twenties. Well, the second step after a hot fling. That was all this weekend could ever be.

She opened her eyes, mind made up. "You're right. There are no guarantees, but I care about you so much and would never hurt you on purpose. Life is short and you, my friend, are the best lover I've ever had."

Grant hissed out a breath. "Oh really? That's funny." He crossed the last cushion, pulled her into his lap, and buried his face in her hair. "Because I care about you so much and you are the best lover I've ever had."

She melted into his embrace, surrendering to the temptation of his touch. "And we need to swear that Toby will never find out. I'd hate for him to feel like we screwed up the Three Musketeers."

Just then, Grant's stomach growled really loud. "Deal. And we need to eat something because obviously I'm starving."

She laughed. "Deal. And if this blizzard ever stops dumping, maybe we can go build a snowman later."

They rose from the couch and returned to the abandoned omelet fixings.

"How about this. Breakfast. Sex. Snowman. Hot tub. Sex. Lunch. Then…" Grant counted off each item on one hand.

She laughed again, her heart lighter than it had felt in ages. "Stop right there. Today's supposed to be spontaneous, right?"

Now that they'd decided sex was on the table––it all felt right.

At least for the next twenty-four hours.

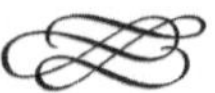

Grant savored the last bite of fluffy, flavorful omelet, set the fork down on his plate, and leaned back in the stool. "That was delicious. Thanks."

Olivia glanced up. "You're on lunch and dinner detail because that's the extent of my repertoire."

"Hey, I know you can cook more than eggs. You cooked for your mom for years."

She nodded. "Yeah, because I had to and I never really did it well, as you know. And it's not really something I want to do. I love to eat and prefer someone else making it." Her full pink lips curved up.

"We have sandwich stuff, right? We'll be okay." The only reason he'd been eating well recently was because his culinary goddess mom cooked dinner.

"I'm not worried." She shrugged. "I can always make us fried eggs. Or scrambled eggs. Or boiled eggs."

He laughed and held up his hands. "Hot tub or shower?"

"Hmm...I think you set the itinerary as sex next? But I think a shower would be an excellent idea. Do you want to go first or should I?" Her ocean-blue eyes widened.

"You mean your shower or mine, right?" Every muscle in his body tightened in anticipation of seeing her satiny skin glistening with moisture again.

The adorable blush pinkened her cheeks—had she always blushed like this or was this a side of her he'd never noticed? Now he knew that rosy flush spread down over her perfect breasts when she was turned on. He sprang to his feet, caught her hand, and drew her to her feet.

"Hey, you almost knocked me over." Her slender fingers dug into his shoulders.

He scooped her up and cuddled her against his chest—this could become a habit. "I've got you and we're going to my shower because it's closer."

She wrapped her arms around his neck and he strode toward his room. "I'm convinced." She turned and brushed her parted lips across his chest. Goose bumps popped up on his skin when she grazed her teeth across his nipple.

He hugged her tighter, a strange feeling of possessiveness slamming into him. She felt so damn natural in his arms—like nothing he'd experienced before. Even with Callie at the beginning of their relationship. What was it between him and Livvie that felt so right? Was it the familiarity and the lifelong history of caring and trust?

Although it was a precarious balance between feeling safe and familiar and dangerous and new. He'd talked a good game earlier about them being able to walk away as friends. Even as his emotions shifted in his chest, he resolved to never tell her. He refused to allow anything to ruin their friendship and if he had to suffer internally, it wouldn't be like it was the first time.

Livvie was embarking on an exciting new chapter in her life, and he wouldn't stand in the way of her finally experiencing adventure. Not after all the plans she'd been forced to give up in her twenties.

So he tucked the blossoming feelings away.

This time with her was worth it.

She was worth it.

Livvie tugged his head down and kissed him, stroking and swirling her tongue against his. The hint of coffee and sweet croissant on her breath tasted delicious. He kicked open the bathroom door without breaking the kiss. He reached the enormous glassed-in shower and relaxed his hold.

She slowly slid down his body, her top riding up, and her impossibly soft skin pressed against him. He groaned and tugged the sweatshirt over her head and yanked her in closer, one hand sliding up to hold her head in place, the other reaching down to cup her perfect ass. She melted against him and leapt up to wrap her legs around his hips. His dick was so damn hard, and when her hot bare flesh rubbed against his, he almost lost it.

Now. He needed to be inside her right now.

She murmured against his mouth, "Take me into the shower. I want to try out that bench." Her hips bucked against him.

They stumbled into the shower together, and he flipped on the faucet, which was blessedly already set at steaming hot. He pressed her against the wall, sliding her up and down his rock-hard erection.

"Here or the bench?" He gritted out the words.

"Let me down." Her words were punctuated by pants and she unwound her muscular legs. She turned and leaned over the bench, bracing her hands against the sculpted stone.

She looked over her shoulder, her eyes heavy, her lips swollen from their kisses, and ran her tongue along her top lip. "I want you to take me from behind. Now."

He growled low in his throat, a primitive heat flaming through him. "Spread your legs and tilt your ass up." He pressed one palm against the curve of her lower back, holding her in place.

He bent down so he was poised at her sweet entrance. His hands curved around her taut hips and in one thrust he slid home.

He held still, savoring the rightness of how they fit together. Like she was made for him. He leaned closer and gently bit the spot where her neck and shoulder met, the way he'd learned made her come apart.

"Grant." She arched her spine up and moaned. "Please."

His jaw clenched and his fingers dug into her hips. "When you ask so nicely."

He started to move, the sensations almost driving him blind. The shower filled with steam, the water pounded on his back, and the world distilled down to their connection.

He'd died and gone to heaven because this level of pleasure couldn't be real.

GRANT TUGGED the fleece throw and tucked it around Livvie's shoulders. After the longest, most satisfying shower of his life, they'd pulled on sweats and planted themselves on the enormous sofa, burrowed into a mountain of pillows and blankets to nap. She spooned in front of him and again; they fit like two puzzle pieces. Which was odd since he was almost a full foot taller than her. But whatever. His eyes closed and he drifted off.

Olivia's husky voice murmured, waking him, "How long have we napped? Did it stop snowing yet?"

He pressed a light kiss on her forehead. "A couple hours. We deserved it. It's still snowing, but more like flurries now."

She snuggled in deeper. "I could stay on this couch all day, but didn't we agree on snow angels? Or a snowman?"

Playing in the snow would be fun. Although, if Grant had his way, they'd just move from the couch to the bed to the counter… An idea popped into his head and he shifted them up to a sitting position.

"Hey, I was comfy." She wrinkled her nose and pushed her bangs off her forehead.

"Let's go build a snowman and I'll shoot some pictures. Maybe Toby can salvage something out of shots of the storm." His camera was gathering dust. Plus, he wanted to photograph Olivia. She was gorgeous and playing in the snow would be the perfect way to capture her effervescent spirit.

"That's a great idea. Even though it is such a bummer about the event. Maybe you can sell some of the photos too, right?" She grinned and rose, holding out a hand.

He accepted her hand and stood. Over the years, he'd forged tons of industry connections. "Definitely. Nature pics are one of the freelance avenues I've been considering. Plus, I was really looking forward to shooting in the snow."

She clapped her hands together and crossed to the kitchen. "Let me throw together a few sandwiches for us while you get your equipment. I'm hungry again."

He laughed. "Me too. We'll need the energy. Hey, will you do me a favor?"

She turned, one dark brow raised. "Sure. You want two sandwiches?"

"One big one is perfect. No, will you wear that red lipstick for me?" He'd already visualized the shots of her bundled up, with only her gorgeous cat-like face showing, her black-fringed blue eyes and scarlet lips the only color in the completely white landscape.

Her mouth dropped open. "You want me to wear a red lip to build a snowman? Seriously?"

"Do it for art. Plus it makes your mouth look..." He caught himself.

Her lips curved into a mischievous smile. "I know what you were going to say. Fine, I'm happy to oblige. Sandwiches first, snow second. And I'll definitely be ready for the Jacuzzi. I'm pretty sure it is positively arctic out there."

He grinned. Of course she'd known what he was going to say. Hopefully they'd test out the theory later. "Perfect."

Feeling relaxed and loose-limbed, he sauntered to his bedroom. When he entered, he halted at the view of the bed, with its tumbled covers and sheets. He shook his head--there was a surreal element about the entire situation, but it was the best reality he'd ever had. The way they could switch from sexy talk to friend talk was incredible. Addictive.

He hunted for his soft box bag that contained his Canon, a few lenses, some speed lights, stands, and a tripod. Not that a tripod worked too well on the slopes, but maybe he could find a spot for it. Eagerness to go outside and play with Olivia spurred him on.

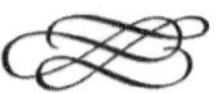

CHAPTER 12

Olivia packed the snow into a tight ball, keeping her back turned to Grant, who was setting up his tripod under the wide deck's awning. The snow had slowed to flurries, but the sky was a mystical pearl gray without any hint of sun. The sensation of being wrapped up in a cloud or some type of dream persisted, emphasized by the preternatural quiet surrounding them. The enormous fir trees were blanketed in snow, just like the world around them. It was breathtaking.

It was also breathtaking because it was freezing. Despite being bundled up with layers of long underwear, wool sweaters, high-tech fabric coat and pants and double insulated socks, she knew she wasn't going to last more than half an hour. Max. Grant was taking his sweet time setting up his camera.

She'd forgotten how fixated and particular he could be with his equipment and his art. They'd had that in common--an attention to detail. Hers was for books and research and art and his in creating unique and beautiful photographs. She'd always been blown away by his talent, even when they were kids.

He'd had an old camera his stepdad gave him and a knack for creating extraordinary images from commonplace objects. When he'd gone to Rochester Institute of Technology and truly gotten into winter sports, he'd struck gold. She wondered if he'd be able to pivot from the adrenaline rush of extreme sports and transition to using his talents in a new way. She hoped so—he had a rare gift.

Gift or not, he was taking too long and her butt was already going numb through her multiple layers of clothing. So, she'd encourage him to pick up the pace. She gave the snowball another pat and admired her handiwork before launching it at his head.

She bit her lip to stifle the laughter bubbling up in her throat when the snowball splatted against the back of his charcoal gray beanie with a satisfying thunk.

He stood still for a moment and slowly pivoted to face her. His brows were drawn into a straight line, his eyes narrowed. "Oh no you didn't."

She snickered. "Hurry up. It's freezing out here. We've got a snowman to build."

He strode toward her, snow adorning his hat and dripping down his face. "You asked for it now."

She turned to run and avoid his retaliation. He grabbed her around her middle and tugged her close against him. She started laughing again. "Come on, it was just in fun. Let's build the snowman. You need to take some photos, right?"

He turned her toward him and lowered his mouth to hers in a quick peck. "Lucky for you I need you as a model. But, when you least expect it, expect it."

The powdery snow that had run down his face tickled her cheeks. She wrapped her arms around him. "That would be so immature of you. Especially since you want to take photos of me with this red lipstick."

"Okay, brat. Camera's ready. Let's make a snowman. I'll do the base and you start on the mid-section, okay? I'll take some shots while you're building, so it looks spontaneous."

"Sounds like a plan." Her cheeks hurt from laughing.

They got to work in companionable silence, rolling and packing the snow. As they each created their portions, Olivia peeked over at Grant. He whistled and his expression reflected his contentment. Whether it was all the recent orgasms or simply being happy, she wasn't sure.

Playing outside was relegating them to familiar territory: the friend zone. Fortunately, his smoking hot body was buried beneath layers of bulky clothing, his broad, long-fingered hands concealed by black gloves. He worked efficiently and quickly, which showcased another one of his admirable traits. She blew out a breath——in her current haze of supreme sexual satisfaction anything and everything he did was admirable.

Regardless, they could still slip into friendship mode and it didn't feel weird. Once they returned to San Diego tomorrow, hopefully they could easily access this camaraderie and their friendship wouldn't suffer even a slight dent.

"Done." He straightened from his crouched position, smacking his palms together to scatter the clinging snow.

His gaze locked with hers and her heart skipped a beat in her chest. Maybe she'd been premature in her assumptions. The minute his tawny eyes met hers, friendship sailed out the window and all she wanted was to kiss him again.

Damn it.

Quite inconvenient.

Forcing her voice to remain even, she replied, "You're speedy. Help me set mine up so we just have to make his head." Keep the focus on fun right now. Although soon they'd return to the hot tub, where it had all begun.

He picked up her contribution and together they adjusted it on the base. "He's going to be perfectly proportioned," Grant said with satisfaction.

Kind of like you. "Well, of course he will. I mean, we're building him, right?" She'd keep it light and fun. Just to prove to herself how easily they could go back and forth from friends to lovers. She could handle it.

Hopefully.

He grinned. "Exactly. Not bad skills for two kids from the beach. You're cool working on his head while I keep shooting?"

She nodded. "Sure." These feelings percolating through her system were just temporary and part of their twenty-four-hour adventure together. She'd spent her twenties planning for the future and sometimes lost sight of being in the moment. She'd savor every second of today and tonight.

He started toward his camera bag and on impulse she called out, "Is my lipstick still perfect?" She pursed her lips into a silly Instagram pout.

He looked back and his eyes hooded. "Livvie. You're so beautiful. Stop teasing me, though. I've got to work."

She stuck out her tongue.

"That's more like it. Child." His expression smoothed out again.

She focused on the snow while he fiddled with his camera and stalked around the perimeter of the property. He was framing a few shots of the surrounding trees and skyline. It was peaceful and gorgeous and it felt like they were the only two people in the world.

She patted and shaped Stevie the snowman's head until it was a round white globe. She walked around the snowman, double-checking for proportions. Satisfied with how the six-foot sculpture had turned out, she reached into her jacket pocket and pulled out the large carrot and dates she'd found in the pantry to improvise his eyes and mouth. She studied the face, determining the proper spot for the nose.

"Livvie."

She glanced up and Grant clicked. "Hey, you could have warned me so I could smile."

"No, I want these to be unselfconscious. Just pretend I'm not here."

She rolled her eyes. Yeah right, because it was so natural to have someone circling you and shooting photos. It wasn't like she hated having her photo taken, but a model she was not. She'd always been the observer, not the subject.

Come to think of it, Grant was the same. Even though he had experienced dozens of countries and cultures and adventures, he was more comfortable as the one documenting, not performing. On the surface, they might look like opposites––world traveler and staid librarian––but inside they had more in common. Probably why they'd been friends forever.

Striving to act unaffected, she dug out a spot and imbedded the snowman's carrot nose. She added eyes and was creating a broad smile when Grant approached. "Look at me."

She turned and grinned. That wasn't too tough. He snapped a few more photos from different angles while she placed the last pieces.

She stepped back, dusted off the snow from her gloves, and perused her handiwork. "All we need is a pipe and a hat. But otherwise, I'd say Stevie is a masterpiece of frozen water. What do you think?"

"Awesome. Okay, turn and strike a pose."

She pivoted and started to lean into the snowman. Before

she realized what was happening, a snowball smacked right into her chest.

Grant hooted and ran backward from her. "Told you to expect it."

She glared and brushed off the snow. "You better not have taken a photo of me getting hit by the snowball." She advanced toward him.

He held up both hands but couldn't stop laughing. "Fair play. And you looked adorable. I'll call that image 'Snowball Surprise' or 'Beauty and the Ball.'"

The fine snow was silent beneath her boots as she stalked him. "That photo will not see the light of day. No way."

He paused and snapped a shot of her. "Stand right there. Think deep thoughts. Aristotle. Plato. Important librarian things."

She snorted, then worked to even out her expression.

"Perfect. Okay, look off toward those trees and visualize you're leaving Athens on a ferry across the Aegean Sea toward Crete."

Her face softened and her lips curved upward. She'd been fantasizing about Greece for so long, especially once she found the collection cataloguing opportunity. Heck, she and Grant shared a love of Greek mythology and history too. Before, she'd pictured herself alone on the turquoise sea, but a visual of Grant leaning against the boat's rail beside her popped into her mind.

She jolted back from her daydream––time to dial back her imagination. The icy wind stung her cheeks, reminding her a Mediterranean idyll this was not. "I can't feel my fingers anymore. I'm ready to go in."

"A few more minutes. Will you make snow angels with me? I think those would make some really cool shots." His dark brows rose.

She exhaled, her breath a white misty puff. "Only for you. And only once. It you don't like how it turns out, too bad."

"Fine. We'll make them right next to each other. A true pair." He moved closer to the line of trees where the snow resembled a white velvet blanket, untouched and pure. He plopped down and gestured to the space to his left.

She joined him. "What about our footprints, won't that mess it up?"

"Nah. That's what Photoshop is for. Let's do this." He lay down, resting his camera on his belly.

She reclined back, ignoring the instant chill from the freezing snow. "Arms and legs, right?" She couldn't remember the last time she'd made a snow angel.

"Yeah. Sweep as big as you can."

While she was ensuring she'd created big wings, he rose. "Okay stay there, I want a picture of you making it too." He snapped away.

"How do I get up without ruining it?" Photoshop couldn't fix everything.

"Draw your arms into your body and take three or four rocks up to seated and press up from there. No hands."

She gathered her momentum and rose. "Aha. It worked." She leapt over the bottom edge of her angel to join him. "Do you want me to help smooth out the snow here at the base?"

"No, I know you're freezing. It'll just take me a second. Go on inside. I'm going to try a few different lenses and then some shots from the deck."

"I'll get a fire started and make some cocoa. See you in a few." She half-ran, half-stumbled to the back of the A-Frame. It was a miracle she didn't face-plant because her toes were numb.

She dashed up the external stairs. She yanked the door open and slammed it behind her. She kicked off the rubber-soled boots, peeled off her snow-covered outerwear, and hung the wet clothes on the hooks in the mudroom. When she pulled off her wool beanie, snow fell onto the sturdy mat floor. Heck, she probably looked just like Stevie the snowman.

She entered the condo, closing her eyes in appreciation of the warmth, so in contrast to the frozen tundra. She did find the mountains stunning, but the older she got, the less appealing being out in the snow became. She paused, contemplating whether she should start the fire first, make the cocoa, or remove the rest of her clothes. She patted herself and found that her inner layers were dry, even though her skin felt frigid beneath the silk long johns and thin wool sweater.

Dry enough to start a fire, which was a priority, even if she planned on submerging herself in the boiling Jacuzzi very soon. She crossed the high wood-beamed-ceiling room to the fireplace. She double-checked the controls and flipped on the gas fire button. Modern technology did not suck.

Cocoa was next. She'd insisted on getting the gourmet dark chocolate brand from the store, along with the giant marshmallows. She didn't have hot chocolate often, but when she did, she insisted on only filling the cup halfway with the hot beverage and stuffing as many marshmallows into the mug as possible.

Grant preferred it the same way. Another thing they had in common.

She located a stainless steel pan to boil the milk and fetched the supplies from the refrigerator and cupboard. She measured out the milk and turned on the heat.

The door flew open and Grant appeared. "Damn it feels good in here."

He shook his head like a puppy, droplets of moisture flying from his shaggy dark hair. He looked so handsome, even with the tip of his nose cherry red and his hair an unruly mop. Nothing could diminish the sparkle in his topaz eyes or the appeal of his lean, square-jawed face.

"Did you get all the photos you'd hoped?"

"We'll look at them together. I know I got some amazing ones of you. Hot chocolate by the fire or in the hot tub?" He set down his camera on the counter and started shucking his clothes.

"Let's have it in here. I want to warm up before I brave that artic breeze again." She poured the steaming hot chocolate into a pair of hot pink mugs with unicorns on them and stuffed as many marshmallows in as she could without capsizing the cocoa.

"Deal." He stepped up behind her and brushed his lips against the nape of her neck, sending shivers down her spine. Even though the tip of his nose was chilly, the rest of Grant emanated a fiery heat. Or maybe that was just her reaction to his proximity.

She handed him his cup and they crossed over to the sofa.

He lounged back into the soft cushions, sampled his cocoa, and beamed at her. "You've always been the cocoa grand master. It's the perfect proportion of marshmallow to chocolate."

She laughed. "Yes, I have. You've got a marshmallow mustache."

He leaned in and kissed her. He pulled back and grinned. "And now so do you."

She shook her head. "You're a five-year-old."

"Yeah, and?" He grinned and gulped down some more cocoa. "It's part of my charm, right?"

"Sure. Whatever you say." Had he and Callie shared the same kind of easy connection?

She tucked her legs beneath her and turned to face him fully. "Not to change the subject from how charming you are, but I wanted to ask you something." Maybe now Grant was relaxed, he'd finally open up more about his marriage.

He gestured with one hand and sipped his drink.

She blew out a breath. "Look, we haven't had time to really talk one-on-one. I can tell you're still sad beneath the surface. Will you tell me what happened with Callie?"

He winced. "Not what I was expecting you to say. Are you sure you don't want to go get naked in the hot tub again?"

Her lips twitched. "I do, at some point. But I'm being serious. It's me, Grant. I want to help and you haven't shared much." She'd do everything in her power to help him resolve the melancholy beneath the lighthearted surface and help him get back on track.

He shifted forward, set down his mug, and rested his elbows on his legs. "What do you want to know?"

"Well, I know you two shared some tragic losses and that she was angry you traveled so much. I know that's a lot, but was there more to your split?"

He dropped his head in his hands. "That's basically it. The miscarriages were heart-wrenching, for both of us. But then everything became about getting pregnant again, like I was just the sperm donor. And by the time we tried IVF, we were basically strangers. Everything was a rigid schedule. And when I made the mistake of saying if it was meant to happen, it would, she lost it. She blamed my travel schedule. Blamed me."

Olivia blinked away the moisture gathering in her eyes. "Oh, Grant, that's not fair. It's not all your fault. Both of you were in the marriage."

He sat up and stared into the fire, one hand massaging the back of his neck. "I don't know anymore. She was right that I loved to travel all the time. And in the end, I never wanted to go back to her because all we did was argue. I thought we loved each other, but maybe we didn't if we couldn't fix our issues."

She scooted toward him and caught his hand, held it with both of hers. "Sometimes love isn't enough. As long as you know you tried your best to make it work, you can't shoulder all the blame. Life doesn't work that way. And…"

He turned to look at her, his eyes bleak. "And?"

"Look, I liked Callie, mostly. When you guys came for Sam's wedding, she never gave you a moment alone. Toby and I both noticed she seemed a little jealous of our friendship. Which was odd." Not to mention that she'd caught Callie giving her the stink eye more than once.

"Seriously? Why didn't you say anything?" His brow furrowed.

"Well, she didn't give us a moment to hang out without her. And you seemed happy and I didn't want to say anything." She lowered her gaze.

"Huh. Maybe she did resent how much I talked about you and Toby. And how frequently we texted and called each other. Which is not okay." He released a harsh breath.

"So if your feelings changed, why have you seemed so sad?" Those shadows beneath his eyes hadn't dissipated.

"I guess I feel like I failed. And now I'm back here, I see how happy my sisters are with their husbands. How amazing marriage can be and I realized I shouldn't have ever married Callie. That maybe she had a point about me not being able to settle down."

She squeezed his hand. "At least you tried. Maybe your version of settling down is different than hers. Maybe she wasn't your person. Please don't believe it was all your fault. It takes two to make a relationship work or fail."

"Yeah, it wasn't like I was a cheating asshole like Toby's dad."

"Of course not. That jerk was in a league of his own."

Olivia slid her arms around him and hugged tight. "You are loyal and caring and a good man, Grant."

He turned and pulled her onto his lap. "I don't want to talk about it anymore. But maybe you have a point that it takes two."

She leaned her head on his broad shoulder. "Thanks for sharing. And speaking of Toby, have you heard from him again? I hope he's not too devastated about the cancellation." And she hoped he wouldn't return to the condo without texting first.

"Nah. I'm sure he and Erin are having fun." Grant's lips quirked.

"As long as he lets us know if he's coming back today." Her tummy clenched.

Grant pressed a kiss on her hair. "He sounded like he was happy to be snowed in with Erin. I don't know about you, but I could use a little nap. Do you want to cuddle up with me?"

"Another nap sounds perfect. Then I'd like to see the photos."

They needed to pace themselves today. A sexy fling was one thing, but they needed to balance it out with their talks and an innocent nap.

Just in case her emotions flared out of control.

Grant stirred on the couch, emerging from sleep slowly, like swimming to the surface from the bottom of the sea. The embers of the fire crackled and popped in the hearth and the buzzing of a telephone was the only other disturbance in the darkened room. Olivia was snuggled in tight to his side, her lips parted in sleep, her chest rising and falling evenly.

He stroked her dark hair away from her face and warmth surged through him. She'd been right, as usual, that he'd feel better if he told her more details about his divorce. Damn, this woman was so special. First as his loyal, lifelong friend, but also as a woman.

It would probably take him the rest of his life to disengage from the physical attraction--if he even could. He would at least hide it from her after tonight.

The phone started up again and this time Olivia stirred. "Need to answer my phone."

She disengaged from his arms and hurried over to her phone. "Damn, three missed calls from my mom." She hissed out a breath.

Grant jolted upright, all vestiges of drowsiness disappearing. Memories of the February when emergency calls came in from the hospital when Livvie's mom had her accident assaulted him. He, Toby, and Livvie had been together at Cardiff Reef after a great surf session, hanging out and enjoying themselves. Any day of the year in San Diego could be a beach day.

Everything had changed in an instant. One moment they were all seventeen and looking forward to college––starting fresh in New York––ready to carve out their own futures. And then that dream ended, at least for Olivia.

"No mom, we're fine. The avalanche was on an uninhabited section of the slopes, nowhere near us. And they canceled the event today because of the whiteout conditions and potential for danger."

Grant rose and walked over to Olivia and started massaging her tense shoulders. At first, she froze and then relaxed back into him, tilting her head to one side to allow him access to the golf-ball-sized knot on her trapezius. He stroked the tight muscles, eager to help.

"Oh, nothing much. Just hanging around the condo. We made some snow angels and built a snowman." She peeked back at him through her thick fringe of lashes, a mischievous glint in her eyes.

She listened for another few moments. "Yes, we'll be careful. We aren't going anywhere today and the roads will be clear for us to drive home tomorrow. Toby's driving since he is the snow expert."

She tensed up again and took a deep inhale.

"No, Toby can't come to the phone right now. Seriously mom, we're in our thirties. We'll call you from the road tomorrow." She nodded. "Yes, of course we'll figure out a time for them to both come to dinner, just like old times."

She set down the phone, gripped the counter tightly, and

blew out a loud exhale. "Seeing those missed calls kicks my pulse up for sure. Oh my god, if she had any idea what we've been doing."

He slid his hands to her shoulders and turned her to face him. He caged her in with his arms. Leaned down for a quick kiss. "Your mom adores me and Toby. Who knows, maybe she'd be excited?" *Or not.*

"I don't know. She thinks of you two as my brothers." Her eyes widened. "It doesn't matter because she'll never know. Nobody will ever know."

Grant's stomach clenched. Unreasonably so. Of course, nobody would ever know. But it felt so right being with her and damn, keeping secrets sucked.

Best to change the subject. "How is your mom handling you going to Greece?" He gazed into her lovely face; her soft mouth was drawn into a tight line.

She shrugged and then stepped in, sliding her arms around his waist and resting her head against his chest. "It's a long story, I won't bore you with it." Her voice was muffled against him.

He stroked one hand down her back and she burrowed in closer, the peach-honey scent of her hair surrounding him. "Hey, earlier you asked me to open up and I feel better. So now it's your turn. Tell me. I hope your mom is supportive about it."

She'd had to grow up too damn fast. Six months after the tragic accident, he and Toby had left for college as planned, leaving Livvie behind.

They'd talked on the phone for hours, especially that first year. So, at least he'd been able to do that. Even if weeks went by between calls, they always picked up where they'd left off. But when he and Toby were at parties or snowboarding at Bristol Mountain, creating connections that changed his life into one long photographic adventure around the world, she'd been helping her mom adjust to a new normal as a paraplegic.

She looked up at him, her blue eyes sober. "To answer your question, last year we had some epic arguments when I was moving out. You were dealing with everything with Callie and I didn't want to add to your stress. My mom was worried at first--she seems to think I'm this sheltered naïve person and couldn't live alone, much less travel alone to Europe. So, I really had to push back. Once we got through that, she's finally happy for my chance to finally start seeing the world."

He frowned. "What? You took care of her for over a decade and she was worried about you taking care of yourself?"

"Right? It was a rough few months, but we're in a good place now." Livvie gave a wry smile.

He stroked her hair back from her face. "You are one of the strongest people I know. And I would have been happy to listen--I'm sorry if it seemed like that wasn't the case."

"You were always there for me." She shifted back and gazed up at him, sincerity shining in her eyes. "I should have told you."

"I am always here for you, no matter what's happening. Our talks were some of my favorite times too. The time change worked perfectly in college--I could come home after a party and it was still early enough to call you. Even if I was a little ripped sometimes." He grinned.

Her lips twitched. "If only I had some recordings. Especially the bad singing." She shook her head. "Anyways, I'm hungry and it's happy hour. How about I pour us a drink, grab the chips and guac, and we look at your pics?"

Reluctantly, he nodded and released her. "I'll grab my camera," he called over his shoulder and strode to his bedroom. He shoved back the unfamiliar stirrings in his chest at her confession she'd not called him when she was having a rough time. He'd make sure that never happened again. Best friends. He'd make the most out of tonight. But he'd pull back and allow her to set the pace.

She'd be the one in the driver's seat for the rest of...whatever this was. He headed into the ensuite bathroom and splashed some cold water on his face. Despite being there for Livvie as her friend, he'd been rock-hard from their hug. Was he going to have this type of physical reaction to his best friend forever?

He was in trouble because he wasn't sure if he'd be able to switch off these feelings as easily as he had the faucet. But he never wanted to cause Olivia any pain––she'd already had enough challenges in her life and he refused to add to it.

He would not add to it.

If she were ready to return to the friend zone, he wouldn't stop her.

Even though he wanted to rip her clothes off and get naked with her all night. He snatched up the camera and strode back into the living room. He hadn't even looked through the shots yet.

While he'd been ruminating, Olivia had turned up the overhead canned lights, cracked open two pale ales, and set up the blue corn chips and a bowl of guacamole on the coffee table in front of the fire. "We're all set up. Bring them over."

"Yes, ma'am." He grinned at her. She was so efficient. He'd been gone less than five minutes and she was already all organized and ready to go. Being a librarian and archivist couldn't be a more fitting career for the most hyper-organized woman he knew.

He sat down next to her but maintained a little space between them. Tonight had to be her leading the way.

He clicked the Canon on and turned so they could scroll through today's frames.

"Wow, how many did you take?" Olivia leaned in closer, her shoulder brushing him, her slender thigh pressing against his.

Hold onto the camera and don't wrap her hair up in your fist and rip off her clothes. "No clue. The more I snap, the more chance for a couple money shots."

"Now that's a fine-looking snowman if I've ever seen one." Livvie saluted him with her beer.

"Yeah, but you steal the shot. This one of you laughing is a keeper." He tilted the camera so she could study it.

"Really?" Her brows drew together over her pert little nose.

"Yeah, really. You radiate happiness and lightheartedness. Everything is crisp and white surrounding you and that red lipstick emphasizes your smile and makes it the center of the photo." And he'd be keeping a copy for himself. Look at it whenever he felt down and realize that she embodied joy.

"Aww. Well, the red does look spectacular, if I do say so myself." She grinned. "I think my mom would love this picture. Especially to have for when I'm gone next year. Oops, I mean this year."

His shoulders tensed, remembering that the tables were turned: he'd be the one staying behind while she set out for adventure. "Yeah, I'll clean it up and get a black 5x7 frame for it." He noted the number on the frame and kept scrolling. Lots of great landscape shots he could choose from later. Some great stock photos of winter mountains and pure snow.

These types of stills were easy income for him, even if they didn't cause his adrenaline to spike like his sports work. He'd been living a nomad's life for more than a decade––he needed to settle down. To see if he was capable of it.

"You're the best. Show me our snow angels." She squeezed his thigh and he stiffened and sucked in a breath.

"Sure." He managed through gritted teeth. Did she not realize what her touch did to him?

She leaned in closer, her entire body pressed against his side. And he had a hard-on. Again.

Six. Five. Four. Three. Two. One. He could control himself. He scrolled through the snow angel photos. "Which one is your favorite?"

Right now they all looked exactly fucking the same to him. Some marks on white snow. He closed his eyes and prayed for control. *Friends. Let her take charge tonight. Please.*

She turned toward him, slid her hand up his thigh, and palmed him. "Um, but I'm pretty distracted by this right now. Can we choose later?"

His eyes rolled back in his head and he collapsed back against the cushions. "Thank god."

"I have something in mind for you. Just lie back and relax." Her voice was low, sexy as hell. She picked up a tube from the coffee table and applied the red lipstick.

He groaned. She yanked down his sweats and his erection sprang free. She wrapped one hand around him and stroked once. Again. If any blood remained in his brain, it shot south now.

"Hmm…take off your shirt please." She wasn't asking. She was demanding and he fucking loved it.

He whipped off his sweatshirt and groaned when she ran her fingernails along his chest and down his stomach, and then took hold of him in both hands.

"Olivia." He held his breath, staring at her in wonder.

"Watch me, Grant. I know what you were thinking about this lipstick." She leaned forward and kissed his cock, never taking her big not-so-innocent blue eyes from his.

He nodded, not trusting himself to speak without sobbing with joy at the vision of her eagerness and her bossiness. No way in hell could he look away now.

Taking her sweet time, she trailed kisses along his hip bone and nibbled her way to the top of his thigh. Teasing. Tasting. Taunting him with the wet heat of her perfect red mouth so close. His hips jerked, the muscles jumping and eager. He gripped the couch cushions with both hands so he wouldn't grab her head and take over.

But if she didn't take him inside soon, he'd be out of his mind. His heart was slamming against his ribs like he was running a marathon. Sweat prickled on his skin and all sensation was located where she gripped him.

"Livvie, please." His back molars were probably ground to dust by now.

She gazed up through dark lashes, her lips curved up. Her eyelids lowered and she murmured, "I'm going to make you come."

She swallowed him in one fast move, taking him all the way until he hit the back of her throat. He bowed up off the couch and his fingers dove into her hair. She set the pace and he won the fucking lottery. Every doubt flew from his brain; hell, every thought had already evaporated. All that remained was searing, pure pleasure.

Grant's lower spine began to prickle and burn. When she added her hand around his base, it sent him flying over the edge with a shout.

Consciousness swam back in and Livvie pressed open-mouthed kisses up his torso until she reached his lips. He pulled her in tight and captured her mouth, her magical talented mouth. This connection was beyond anything he'd ever experienced.

With his best friend.

After a moment, she pulled back and gazed up at him, her expression soft. "I'm starving now. Will you make your spaghetti carbonara? We got all the ingredients, right?"

He laughed. "Right now, I would make you anything you want. But are you sure I can't return the favor first?"

He stroked his hand down and curved it around her hip.

She shook her head and disengaged. "No, I like having the upper hand for right now. And I'm seriously starving. Playing in the snow and napping builds an appetite."

His skin was cold where she'd been pressed against him, but he grinned at her playfulness. "Me too. But you might have to help me stand up. My knees are weak."

She laughed and tugged on his hand. "Come on, pull up your pants, leave the shirt off, and feed me. Feed me dinner, that is." She winked.

He rose from the couch to join her, adjusting himself back into his sweats. "Well, if I'm going shirtless, it's only fair you do too, right?"

"How about I'll go bottomless? Deal? I mean I've already got the sweatshirt and big socks on." She gestured down to her toned, spectacular legs.

"Deal. Have a seat at the bar and I'll whip everything up." He headed toward the kitchen.

"I'll clean up the chips and then I've got a playlist I made for us––it's going to bring you back to high school. All our favorites."

"Awesome." Grant ignored the twinge in his chest. Tonight was it. Would reminiscing about the good old days and their friendship make it awkward? Or emphasize how damn compatible they were?

CHAPTER 14

Olivia busied herself fastening the chip bag closed and cleaning up the coffee table while Grant hustled around the kitchen. She was trying to get her hormones under control so they could have a regular dinner together. Was their connection so intense because they knew each other so well or because they trusted each other beyond measure or because their chemistry simply was just that explosive?

Not that she planned on depriving herself of more earth-shattering sex tonight. But twelve hours from now, they'd be packing up the SUV to head back to San Diego. With Toby.

Attempting to act like nothing had changed.

As she collected the dishes, she glanced over her shoulder, impressed at the sight of Grant simply plucking a bottle of olive oil from a tall cabinet. Naturally graceful in all his tawny glory. Finding the balance of separating their physical connection and their lifelong friendship promised to be a challenge. She and Grant had always shared an undefinable bond, an easy compatibility.

Tonight was about romance and finishing their time

together with a bang--she silently snickered, no pun intended. Plenty of time to worry about repercussions later. She crossed the room and ran one hand down his solid back. "Do you need any help? Want me to chop anything or…?"

He shook his head and smiled down at her. "No, this is one of the few meals I've got down. Why don't you relax?"

If she sat and watched him cook with all those defined muscles rippling, she'd overheat before the water boiled for the spaghetti. Nope, she needed to distract herself for the next few minutes.

She smirked to herself. She needed a solid dinner to fuel the rest of the evening.

"You know what, I'll go organize all our gear in the garage so it's ready to go. I know Toby wants to leave early to avoid traffic. We don't need a repeat of that slowdown that we hit on the way up."

He nodded and gathered bowls for the pasta, cheese, pancetta, and salt and pepper. "Yeah, you're right. That'd be great."

She grabbed Toby's key fob and her coat and entered the garage. She double-checked their gear hanging on the wall racks and everything was blessedly dry. Their snowboard boots and helmets were strewn in a haphazard pile beneath them.

She shook her head. Both Toby and Grant had always been messy little pigs. She'd thought they'd grow out of it once they became adults, but everything was dumped in heaps just like when they'd been teens. The guys had teased her about being a control freak with her obsessive need for order and they were probably right. Being excessively neat was quite helpful in her chosen profession, thank you very much.

And her tumultuous childhood with her loving, but disorganized single mom and subsequent role as a caretaker at seventeen had cemented her need for ruthless organization. She simply felt better when everything was in place. And she wasn't alone. Hadn't everyone seen the big trend toward the life benefits of ridding your home of clutter? Feng shui and all that?

Organizing stuff relaxed her. And since her attraction for Grant was simmering beneath her skin, poised to blast through the surface, she needed to keep her hands busy for now. It only took fifteen minutes to pack their snowboarding gear into the back of Toby's SUV. She surveyed the now tidy space, brushed her damp palms on her thighs, and paused at the closed door.

She turned the doorknob and went inside. Time for dinner and fun. "I'm home, honey, is dinner ready yet?" She sang the words.

His lips twitched. "Just like you to come home when everything is ready. We're five minutes away from the best pasta you've ever tasted. Will you open the wine?"

It was all so domestic. So normal. They'd eaten meals together since they were kids. This one would be different.

She strolled up to him and lifted onto her tiptoes to kiss his cheek, enjoying the scratch of his dark scruff. "Of course. I'm going for the Rhône blend if that's cool with you?"

"Perfect. I'll plate it and we're ready to go."

She opened the wine and when she returned to the island where they'd set up their places, he was skillfully sprinkling fresh parmesan on the pasta.

Her mouth watered. "Okay, I'm drooling. This looks amazing. When did you learn how to make this? It looks like a professional chef put it together."

"On one of the trips to Italy, a few of the crew and I took a cooking class in Tuscany. This woman Juliana had her own property with olive trees, vineyards, and a kitchen to offer group classes. We made all the food under her supervision and then got to eat it outside under a pergola."

Olivia sighed. "Oh my god, that sounds like a dream--*Under the Tuscan Sun*--right? Italy is at the top of my list."

He brushed his fingers along her cheek. "You'll love it there. It's beautiful, everyone is nice, and the food is the best in the world. Everything is so fresh--no chemicals in the food supplies. Even all the gluten-free, dairy-free peeps could eat the bread and pasta and pizza."

"I always think if I had to give up bread I'd be devastated. Or cheese. Or pizza. I could seriously eat it every single day for the rest of my life." She turned and pressed her lips against his palm.

"Well, we had pizza yesterday so here's your pasta. A slice of Italy in the California mountains." He waved one hand at the dishes and lifted his glass with the other.

She clinked his raised glass. "To delicious food with my favorite person in the world."

Grant Michaels *was* her favorite person in the world. She wouldn't be who she was today without the foundation of their friendship. They were basically the perfect pair. Best friends. Loyal. Generous. Caring. Solid. And physically…her heart skipped a beat.

"You're my favorite person too." His eyes darkened as their gaze caught over the rim. "Nothing can ever change that."

"Never." A chill shot down her spine.

"Let's eat. I'm starving." He twirled some of the creamy pasta around his fork, turning his attention to the steaming dish.

She sampled her first bite. Her eyes drifted shut in pleasure as a delicate blend of flavors exploded on her tongue. The creamy sauce--not too heavy--the savory pancetta, mixed with the crisp parmesan and exact perfect accent of cracked pepper. She moaned and chewed slowly, prolonging the exquisite taste.

When she opened her eyes, he was staring at her, his eyes hooded. "Okay, that was like something out of *When Harry Met Sally*. I'm not going to make it through the entire meal if you react like that."

Her lips curved up. "I've always been noisy when I eat. Never bugged you before. Hmmm...I wonder what's different?" She speared another bite and batted her eyelashes.

His brows drew together, but he laughed. "How did I not know you were such a little brat?"

"Moi?" Laughter bubbled up in her throat.

He leaned in and gave her a quick kiss. "Yes, you. I guess before I associated those moans and groans with you loving food and now I know you make those sounds when I'm inside you, so..."

Whoa. Heat flooded her cheeks and she cleared her throat. "Um..."

"Don't get shy on me now, Livvie." He continued eating his dinner, all cool and nonchalant.

While she prided herself on being able to handle the sexy times, somehow it felt different with him talking dirty at dinner. Her earlier bravado fled. Olivia shifted on her stool, heat pooling in her belly, and a flurry of nerves skittering across her skin.

He set down his fork and angled toward her, sliding one hand along her thigh, trailing heat with his fingertips. "You okay?"

She nodded, then reached down and intertwined her fingers with his. "It's like you said. One minute it's just you and me, two of the Three Musketeers and then, boom. I don't know if my brain has caught up to what my body is feeling. If that makes sense."

He squeezed her hand and his gleaming golden eyes

searched hers. "It makes perfect sense. We're both winging it."

The knot in her chest softened. "You're better than me at turning it on and off. I hope I don't slip up tomorrow with Toby and call you love muffin or something."

He snorted. "Love muffin? Toby would veer off the road and hit a tree. And I don't think I could handle that moniker without laughing. How about stud? I'd answer to that."

Now it was her turn to snort. "Stud? More like nerd."

He slid off the stool, stepped between her thighs, and pulled her in close. Her laughter evaporated as her pulse raced and her center flamed. "You're the sexiest nerd I've ever met. Wrap your legs around me." Grant's voice was husky.

Dinner forgotten, she obeyed his demand, tightening her legs around his narrow hips. "I thought I was the boss?" Although right now she'd do whatever he asked.

He captured her mouth, stroking his tongue along hers, the taste of red wine and parmesan on his warm breath. "Tell me what you want." His voice rumbled in his throat.

A shiver of excitement shot down her spine and she rocked her pelvis against the stiff ridge of his erection. "I want what you just suggested. I want you inside me. Now."

He growled and gripped her ass and pressed against her. "Where."

She wrapped her arms around his powerful neck. "The fireplace rug. And I want to be on top."

In a split second, he'd landed them on the sheepskin rug in front of the crackling fire. Somehow he rolled them so he was on his back and she was astride him. He crossed his arms behind his head and gave a devastating grin. "I'm all yours."

For a moment, she stared down at the magnificent creature beneath her. She whipped off her sweatshirt, placed her hands on his square pecs and leaned down. "No more talking."

She pressed her lips against his and her brain flipped off. Now was time for sensation and she planned to revel in every single one. He slanted his mouth across hers, deepening their kiss to a frenzied intensity, with tongues and teeth clashing. Her breasts smashed against him and the sensation of his smooth skin against hers drove her wild.

She was ready. Eager. Couldn't wait another moment.

She sat back and yanked his sweatpants down, so no barriers remained between them. The scratch of his leg hair against her thighs, his rigid length lined up with her center, the sensual power coursing through her veins. Tomorrow everything would change, but tonight...tonight he was hers.

His square jaw was tense and his white teeth dug into his lower lip. Their gazes remained locked, his eyelids heavy over pupils so dilated his eyes were fathomless. No longer golden, but dark and mysterious. She lifted her hips and grasped him in one hand, braced herself on his solid chest with the other. Slowly, oh so slowly, she lowered herself onto his cock, inch by inch until they were fully connected.

He groaned or maybe she groaned. She couldn't tell any longer where he began and she ended. Her eyes drifted shut and she savored the fullness, unable to move from the perfect fit.

"Olivia," he rasped and his hips jerked upward.

She opened her eyes and shifted forward, experimenting until she found the perfect angle. "Give me your hands."

He reached up and interlaced their fingers, his callused palms sparking chills down her spine. She folded forward until their linked hands pressed into the fluffy rug next to his shoulders. Her breasts hovered inches above his chest and the heat from his skin melded with hers. She crossed the space between them and dove in for another kiss.

With tongues tangling and the sweat prickling on their joined bodies, she began to move. Each stroke, each breath filled her with a pleasure she'd never known, a connection she'd never experienced. A desire beyond any she'd encountered. She stared into his handsome face, so familiar and so dear, but with his hooded eyes, his parted lips, his harsh breath, he was another Grant.

He joined her rhythm, his hands sliding down to grasp her hips and encourage her pace. She rose above him, her hands fisting in her hair, and lost herself in him.

For tonight, nothing else mattered but this passion, this feeling, this connection.

CHAPTER 15

Olivia woke with a start, her skin chilled, her thoughts jumbled. She blinked the sleep from her eyes and bolted upright when she registered the time on the wall clock.

"Crap. Wake up." She shook Grant's shoulders. "It's six. Toby could be back any minute."

Soft pre-dawn light filtered in through the French doors, revealing the makeshift bed she and Grant had constructed on the sheepskin rug, after round two—or was it round three?—last night. Fear propelled her to her feet and she shoved her tangled hair out of her face. She had total sex-all-night bedhead and if that wasn't a clear giveaway, in addition to them being bare-ass naked, nothing else was. Grant moaned and turned over, dragging the pillow over his head.

She kicked him, well, just a little toe tap. "Get up, lunkhead. Toby."

Her words must have infiltrated his drowsiness because he popped up to sitting. "What? What time is it?" He scrubbed at his disheveled hair, a slight frown tugging down his lips.

"Six. Toby will be back any minute. We need to clean up and make sure everything looks normal, and us naked in the living room is not normal." Panic threaded through her voice and adrenaline fueled her trot toward the stairs.

"Hey, not even a good morning kiss?" Grant grumbled.

She glanced back and paused at the sight of him rubbing his eyes. Damn, he was adorable. He had never been a morning person and truth be told, they hadn't gotten much sleep last night.

Regret gnawed at her––she'd love to kiss him again, but that portion of the weekend program was completed. Time to return to reality and now. "No. Remember. Best friends. Toby. Chop-chop. I'm hopping in the shower and so should you."

"Fine. I'll put on some coffee." He didn't budge.

She dashed up the stairs and slammed her bedroom door behind her. She leaned forward, gripped her thighs, and struggled to regulate her breathing. Her heart was racing like she'd hiked up one of Mammoth's vertical peaks instead of jogged up one flight of stairs.

Glimpses from the last forty-eight hours with Grant danced behind her closed eyes. The laughter, the passion, the connection. Her hammering pulse accelerated, a painful drumbeat in her temples as the realization swept through her––she loved him.

Not just loved him like she had since she was twelve years old but loved him loved him. Like *in love* with him. Her knees buckled and her strength sapped out of her suddenly, like she was a marshmallow––squishy and soft. She sank to the floor, the sturdiness of the door behind her ensuring she didn't collapse.

No, no, no, no. Damn it, why? She dropped her forehead to her knees and wrapped her arms around her shins and squeezed. Why couldn't she have just enjoyed the sex and reverted back to best friend mode?

Probably because she hadn't shared such profound intimacy before. Between caring for her mom and finishing college and grad school, she'd kept most of her relationships casual. Tinder swipes and all that. A few of the guys she'd dated for longer than a few months wanted too much of her time and she simply hadn't had the bandwidth.

Besides, she'd always planned to go abroad and didn't want to risk a significant other holding her back. Not the way circumstances had held her back during her twenties. In two months, she'd be leaving for an entire year. He was back in California to settle down. Even if somehow Grant felt the same way and they decided to give it a shot, a friendship could be maintained via video chat and phone calls, but a romantic relationship could not. It was impossible.

And this was assuming Grant felt the same way.

No, there was nothing to be done but to pull herself together and act like nothing had happened. She half-stumbled to the bathroom, her legs still shaky and her mind whirling. Her brain shifted into autopilot. Shower. Get dressed. Go downstairs and pour a mug of coffee the size of her head, and pack.

A clanking and loud voices downstairs alerted her Toby was back. She exhaled an unsteady breath and flipped on the shower faucet, directly to blazing hot. Thank god she'd made it upstairs before he returned. If she hadn't woken up when she did ten minutes ago, the ride home to San Diego would have been tense, at best.

She realized she'd run upstairs naked and her sweatshirt was somewhere in the living room. Oops. She stepped into the steamy spray, allowing the pummeling of the water to act as a wake-up call. In every way. Reaching for the shampoo, she switched her mind to the tasks at hand, blocking out everything else.

By the time she descended the stairs, she'd once again be Olivia Hanlon, Toby and Grant's best friend.

∾

"What the hell? Whose bathing suit is this?" Toby yelled from the deck, a bikini bottom dangling from one hand.

Grant grimaced. *Oh shit.* Olivia was still upstairs so he had to react fast. "It has to be Livvie's because nobody else was here."

Toby walked through the French doors and dropped the sopping wet material onto the kitchen counter. His eyebrows were raised up to his hairline and his eyes narrowed. "Well, that's strange."

Grant managed to keep his face expressionless. "Dude, we were drinking. Maybe she took it off when she put on her robe out there. I dunno. Good thing you found it though." He forced a short laugh.

Toby stared at the counter. Livvie came bounding down the stairs, duffle bag in hand. "I'm ready to go as soon as I have coffee."

"Aren't you forgetting something?" Toby pointed to the wet scrap of material.

"Huh?" Livvie stared at the counter and the color drained from her face. "Is that my…"

"You must have tossed it back when you put on your robe, right? Good thing Toby checked or the owners would have a little surprise." Grant's voice was too cheery in his own ears, but he couldn't seem to shut up.

Color rose in her cheeks as fast as it had disappeared. "Oh yeah, you're right." She nodded and picked up the suit. "Yeah, you know I hate wet bathing suits. I must have been more buzzed than I thought. Silly me."

Toby looked between them and scratched his cheek. "You two are acting weird. Something up?"

"Just a little hungover. Sorry." Olivia kept her gaze down and rifled through the kitchen drawers until she found a plastic bag to house her damp swimsuit.

"Whatever. Let's jam out of here in the next twenty minutes, deal?" Toby shrugged and headed up the stairs to his room.

"Livvie," Grant hissed.

She met his gaze and shushed him. "Thanks for making coffee, Grant. I'll clean out the pot and I'm ready." Her voice was louder than usual, her tone friendly and normal.

He gritted his teeth. She was right, they needed to act like everything was just the same as when they'd left the New Year's Eve party. Squaring his shoulders, he strode to his room to pack and officially screw his head on straight.

Twenty minutes later, Grant slammed the back of Toby's Land Rover and climbed into the passenger seat. Olivia had chosen to sit in the back, claiming she had some paperwork to review on the ride home. Which he knew was bullshit.

After the close call with Toby, he'd play it cool and detach over the long drive. He felt itchy and frustrated and out of sorts. Not a promising start to returning to "friendship" with Livvie.

Toby navigated down the now clear streets, framed on either side by packed walls of dirty snow. Grant stared out the window, the murky gray sky mirroring the heavy dullness filling him. Although the colorful passionate images of he and Olivia together were etched inside him, the reality of returning to real life depressed him.

"Hey, can you find us some music? It's too damn quiet in here," Toby said.

Grant shook himself back to the present. "Yeah, sorry. Of course." He fiddled with the radio and Bluetooth.

Without asking, Olivia handed him her phone. "Hit the Ride Home Playlist. Should be upbeat--a lot of Foo Fighters and Fitz and the Tantrums."

A grin split Toby's face. "Yeah. Perfect."

"It's the least I could do. And hey, I'm so sorry about the event. I know you were really counting on this one. Stupid snowstorm." Livvie's slender hand squeezed Toby's shoulder.

And now Grant was remembering her hand gripping him. Everywhere. He shifted uncomfortably in his seat. He hit Play and Dave Grohl's voice howled about not wanting to be your monkey wrench.

Fitting lyrics. He couldn't be an obstacle to Livvie's plans. Wouldn't. She deserved the chance for freedom and adventure, just like he and Toby had experienced.

Toby shrugged. "Well, the good news is that the donors insisted on me keeping the money, even without the expo happening. Conditions are conditions, right? But it sucks because the riders and spectators were looking forward to it. And I really needed some fresh photos for the website. But I'll figure it out."

"Oh, Grant got some great photos--maybe not boarding ones, but at least some winter shots, right?" Livvie said.

"Yeah, well, we built a snowman and made some snow angels. There are some cool shots with Livvie and some solid winter background stills. At least the blizzard is document-ed." *And nothing from what happened the rest of the time, thankfully.*

"Sounds like you two had fun while being snowed in. And yeah, if you got some pictures documenting the epic blizzard, those could work for a story about why the expo didn't happen." Toby nodded, his fingers drumming on the steering wheel.

Livvie drew in a sharp breath and Grant shifted in his seat again. No way could Toby ever discover just how much fun they'd had together.

"Yeah, we had a snowball fight and I won. As usual." Livvie bragged from the backseat. Perfect distraction. Bring it back to their regular playful buddy dynamic.

Toby laughed. "Of course you did. Got him when he was setting up the camera, right? Works every time."

"Glad you guys find it so funny. That's expensive equipment I've got and it's all fun and games until someone loses a lens." Grant's lips twitched. In retrospect, it had been funny.

Livvie groaned. "Oh my god, no puns. Please."

"So, I can't believe neither of you have asked about the rest of my weekend." Toby quirked a brow.

"Just didn't have a chance yet--we've got hours. But yes, do tell." Olivia's voice carried a hint of strain beneath the forced lightness. At least he could hear it. And hoped Toby couldn't.

"Probably a different kind of fun than you two. I'm seeing Erin again tomorrow night." A small smile played around Toby's mouth.

Grant lightly punched his buddy's shoulder. "Wow. Already have a date. This sounds serious." Toby had only had a few serious relationships. His first love had broken his heart and the second one had ended up screwing her boss, who was not Toby. Added to his issues surrounding his dad, Toby kept things superficial.

"Do tell." Olivia leaned in toward Toby's seat.

"I don't know. She's special. Different. And being snowed in forced us to get to know each other faster. She sure as hell is cooler than anyone I've met in the last few years." Toby shrugged a shoulder.

"That's so exciting. I'm happy for you," Olivia said and promptly reclined back against the seat cushions.

Toby shrugged again. "It's early, but it's just easy with her. Sorry you two didn't get the chance to hookup."

Grant choked on the swallow of coffee he'd just taken. He managed to stuff the cup back into the holder and leaned forward, struggling to stop coughing.

Toby smacked him on the back a few times. "Hey man, you okay?"

"Yeah, went down the wrong pipe." He held up one hand and wheezed, still unable to catch his breath. Shit, at this rate, the ride home would kill him. Time for some safer topics of discussion. Or maybe he needed to stop relating everything Toby said to him and Olivia's sex marathon.

Olivia piped in from the back. "Remember I'm leaving in a couple of months for Greece, so I'm not looking to meet anyone new."

But you sure enjoyed being with someone old. Grant could finally breathe again and picked up his coffee. How had he believed this would be easy? Why the hell had he convinced her they should extend their one night romp?

Because now she was imprinted on him––not just as one of his favorite people in the world, but as the best lover. No easy way to separate out his emotions. But he needed to figure it out because he was back in San Diego to stay now.

And Livvie would be here, at least for the next few months. They'd all planned on spending time together as best friends––the Three Musketeers. It would be one thing if she were leaving in a week. Then, they'd have the built-in separation from being thousands of miles apart and he'd be able to lick his wounds in private and act like her best friend.

His shoulders tensed and his throat tightened. But that wasn't happening. For the next two months, they'd be hanging out and he'd have to act like everything was the same as it had been when they'd arrived in the mountains.

"So is it for sure?" Toby asked.

"Unless something unusual happens, my boss confirmed I was a shoo-in. Apparently, there aren't too many archivists ready for restoration work available to leave the country for a full year."

"I'm so stoked for you. I haven't been to Greece before, but I heard it's amazing. Will you be in Athens the whole time or do you get to see the islands?" Toby asked.

"Crete or Rhodes, right?" Grant said. He'd always wanted to visit Crete or the Dodecanese Islands, where Rhodes was located. Ever since his dad had given him a book on Greek mythology when he was in elementary school, he had loved the history, the mythology, the culture. Somehow in all his meandering, he hadn't visited yet.

"Yes, so I think Keri, my boss, said that I'll get one of two positions either in Rhodes or Crete." She clapped her hands together. "I can't believe it's finally happening. I don't care which one. And I get to spend a few weeks in Athens either way."

"Who knows, maybe Grant and I could come over. The three of us have never gotten to travel internationally together before. You can be our tour guide," Toby said.

Grant's gut tightened. The three of them. That's the unit they were. And had to remain. Maybe in several months, his feelings would change. Maybe he was just on a mountain high, especially after such a shitty year.

"That would be awesome. We'd have a blast." As long as he could handle it.

Olivia hesitated for a split second before responding. Did Toby notice or was Grant just hyper-sensitive to every single thing she did now? Grant gripped his thighs, digging his fingers into the muscles to remind himself not to say or do anything stupid.

"I'd love that. It all seems like a dream." Livvie sighed.

"Don't get swept off your feet by some Greek god or

anything. I hear those guys are jealous. Wait until we come." Toby joked.

"You're a goof. Nobody's ever come between us before and I can't imagine that ever happening." She swatted Toby's shoulder and slid a sideways glance at Grant. Her blue eyes were guarded.

Toby held out his fist, Olivia lifted hers, and Grant reluctantly joined in the three-way fist bump. "All for one and one for all."

"Love you guys. And Grant, thanks again for offering to help me out. Sorry it didn't work out how we planned and I hope you're not mad I stayed with Erin, but hopefully you two had a good time."

Grant nodded. "We had a great time." *Dude, you'll never know how great.*

Livvie echoed him. "A great time."

"Well, let's make a plan for next weekend. I'm heading out of town after that for a few weeks and want to hang as much as possible before Livvie jets off. Surf and grill out or something?" Toby asked.

Grant rubbed the iron-tight muscles on the back of his neck. "Sounds good."

Livvie donned her reading glasses and adjusted her noise-canceling headphones. "Absolutely. Okay guys, I've got to spend a little time with these papers. I'll check back in a few hours."

Grant and Toby looked at each other and cracked up. Their librarian friend was returning to full introvert mode. When she dove into a book or research, she was capable of tuning out the entire world. He needed to tune out too.

"You cool with me grabbing a quick nap? I can drive later." All the tension from acting like everything was status quo was exhausting.

"Sure, no problem. Just make sure the music is queued up."

Grant cranked up the stereo. He let his head fall back on the headrest and closed his eyes. Maybe when he awoke, he wouldn't be reliving the feel of Olivia's silky skin beneath his hands or the feel of being buried inside her heat.

Like he could ever forget.

CHAPTER 16

Olivia stared at the computer screen, rereading the same paragraph until the words resembled squiggly caterpillars instead of painstakingly crafted academic text. While she loved her work, sometimes the esoteric nature of some of the articles and educational pamphlets fried her eyeballs. There was always the writer who apparently believed they were paid by the syllable. They rejoiced in creating page-long sentences, even if it rendered the information indecipherable.

Enough. She leaned back in her ergonomic office chair, whipped off her reading glasses, and massaged the bridge of her nose. Sure, the article on twenty ways to spice up academic research papers was likely contributing to her short-circuiting brain. The crux of it, however, lay in her mind's annoying ability to play what she was calling the "Grant Reels" on auto-repeat.

Grant laughing, his expression open and lighthearted. Grant eating pasta with his usual gusto for food. Grant shredding down the mountain, snowboarding like a pro. Grant's amber eyes full of passion the moment before his mouth slanted across hers. Grant reclining back in bed, his eyes hooded. Grant on the couch, his rough, wide palms skating along her skin. Grant in the Jacuzzi, his muscles gleaming in the dim light.

Grant. Grant. Grant.

Yup, Grant on the brain. It had been three days since they returned to San Diego and she couldn't exorcise the memories they'd created. They'd survived the ride back without arousing Toby's suspicion, but tomorrow could be a challenge. They were planning on horseback riding and grilling out with the McNeills, Grant's extended family. Originally, they'd planned on surfing down at Black's Beach and dinner at Pacific Vista Ranch because Angela, Grant's mom, wanted to see them all together.

In an unusual turn, the latest winter storm had bypassed them and the Pacific Ocean, usually filled with pumping waves this time of year, was placid as a lake. Farther up the California coast, the waves were at least head high, but not at home. So, they'd switched gears. Olivia hadn't been on a horse in years, so that would probably be amusing––at least for any observers.

Pacific Vista Ranch, where Grant moved as a teenager with his mom and brothers, was a rambling horse breeding ranch, a mere five miles from the beach. The rolling emerald hills and breathtaking vistas were something to behold. The first time Grant had invited her and Toby over, they'd been blown away. All three of them had been raised strictly middle-class and had never seen anything like the McNeill's sprawling estate, three enormous guesthouses, stables to house more than a hundred horses, a racetrack, and more.

Chris McNeill, Angela's second husband, was Hollywood royalty––a director/producer who'd left Los Angeles after a tragic accident left him a widower. Chris never tried to replace the Michaels boys' father, but he cared for them like they were his own. Olivia had sometimes imagined if she had a dad, he'd be strong and kind like Chris.

Angela was an incredible chef and loved nothing more than to have her family and friends gathered around the table. Her hospitality was legendary. She'd also been supportive when Olivia's mom had her accident and Olivia loved her like a second mom. No way would she refuse an invitation to the ranch.

But she and Grant hadn't seen each other since Mammoth. Beyond a few brief group texts that included Toby, they hadn't communicated. Was he as obsessed as she was or had he already buried the weekend into his mind's deep vault and tossed away the key?

Her phone rang. Welcoming the distraction, she answered. "Hey, Mom."

"Hi Livvie, Rose is making her epic vegetarian chili and cornbread tonight. Come on over, we both want to hear about Mammoth."

She pursed her lips, unsure if she could pull off a nonchalant description of the weekend yet. "Well I'm still at work––"

"Livvie, it's almost five on a Friday. Soon you're going to be thousands of miles away drinking ouzo and eating baklava. Please?" Nothing like a mild guilt trip.

Her gut tightened. Two more people to hide the truth from. Now that she no longer lived with her mom, she missed her. Even though, over the years when she'd been her sole caretaker and Rose had lived across the country, she'd wished for nothing more than her freedom.

Time to start acting like everything was fine. "You're right. I'm not going to get any more work done tonight." Not that she'd accomplished much today.

Would these feelings for Grant settle or when she saw him again on Saturday would they be different? Maybe she was romanticizing it all. The sexy snowed-in weekend seemed like a dream.

She confirmed the time for dinner and powered down her computer. In a few months, she wouldn't have the opportunity to drop in for dinner with her mom. Everything was about to change. Nobody to worry about but herself. No responsibilities besides work. No duties. No resentment. No guilt and shame over said resentment. *Ha.*

It wasn't like her fiercely independent mom had wanted to rely on her teenaged daughter and require help with tasks that used to be routine before the accident. Hell, her mom had raised her solo, while often juggling two jobs. During the first few years of recovery, her mom simply needed the help. Physical and occupational therapy made a big difference, but it took time for her mom to regain her confidence in her ability to be autonomous. Olivia probably could have moved out after the first few years, but by that point, it just made sense for her to stay.

Why would they pay for part-time help when Olivia could do it? Her college was in La Jolla and her Master's program was online. They'd adopted Java, a black lab service dog, who became not just her mom's protective companion, but Olivia's honorary little sister.

When Aunt Rose's circumstances changed and she offered to move from Maryland to live with Olivia's mom, Olivia rented a sweet little studio cottage in Solana Beach. She loved living alone and eating cereal for dinner or not having dinner at all. Doing whatever she wanted. But she did miss her mom.

She stuffed her aluminum water bottle and smartphone into her daffodil yellow satchel, then wrapped her cheerful tomato-red scarf around her neck. Sure, it was January in San Diego and it was fifty-nine degrees and sunny. A huge improvement over the frigid climate up in the Sierra Nevada mountains.

But for Southern Californians, this was chilly winter weather. These were the same people who cried for air conditioning when the needle moved beyond seventy-five. Her lips twitched--most people would be wearing ski jackets, UGGs, and wool beanies right now. At least she only wore a cardigan over her outfit.

She flicked off the light and exited her closet of an office. Maybe spending time with her mom and Rose would help her stop ruminating about Grant. At least for the next few hours.

GRANT CLOSED his eyes and groaned as the hot water sluiced over his weary muscles, offering a brief respite from the ache in every damn one of them. Breeding season was in full swing at the ranch and his stepsister Sam was killing him slowly. Of course, she worked harder than anyone as the horse breeding manager and ranch manager. The problem was she expected everyone to labor like she did--nonstop. Not that he was a slacker, but ranch work and foaling was intense.

A major change of pace from taking pictures, which was more mentally challenging or exhilarating depending on the shoot. Sure, he had to be agile and fast to capture the athletes and handle equipment, but nothing compared to working with horses.

He scrubbed his scalp with the fresh-scented shampoo, working to remove what felt like an inch of dirt stuck in his hair. The Santa Ana winds had kicked up today and he may as well have rolled around in the soil instead of striding through it. For now, working on the ranch was exhausting him mentally and physically, which helped him stay grounded until he had a plan in place for his next move.

He'd sent out some emails to his contacts in the surf industry to see about shooting a few competitions or brand campaigns. Nothing long-term––there were tons of opportunities in SoCal that he could drive to for the day or overnight. He'd even consider video work, as long as it didn't require signing on to full tours.

One thing the work didn't do was distract him from memories of last weekend with Olivia. As he grabbed the soap, a flash of her all slick and slippery in the shower with him caused his body to throb with need. Damn it, she'd be here tomorrow with Toby. How would he be able to act like it was the Three Musketeers as usual?

On one hand, life would be a hell of a lot simpler if the weekend hadn't happened. Not to mention all the icy showers he could have avoided since he'd been home. But the rest of him, most of him if he were honest with himself, never wanted to erase the most incredible hours of his life. Olivia was the most compassionate, loyal, brilliant person he'd ever met. She deserved to spread her wings and have the chance to explore the world and choose a worthy man.

She deserved the best. Not a guy with a failed marriage and no career.

Flipping off the shower, he opened the glass door and grabbed his towel. Dinner was in fifteen minutes up at the house and he was freakin' starving. No way could he sustain the breeding season pace without the hearty meals his mom made. After living his twenties on the road, belonging part to the McNeill/Michaels clan was comforting.

He pulled on a clean pair of jeans, threw on a flannel, and strode out the door. His mom hated tardiness so he half-jogged up the path to the main house, ignoring the tightness in his lower back.

His phone pinged when he entered the enormous wooden front door. He fished it out of his back pocket and frowned. Callie. He hadn't heard from her in months and it was early morning in Australia——probably not casual news. He strode down the wide hallway toward the kitchen, and his jaw tightened when he opened the email.

It was official. They were divorced in the eyes of the law now, not just through their physical and emotional separation. He exhaled a jagged breath and halted just shy of the broad doorway. He skimmed the document, complete with the declaration, official seal, and effective date. He leaned against the wall, dropped his head back against the cool hard surface, and massaged the iron-tight muscles of his neck. His mind went numb.

He was the only person in his family who'd ever been divorced. He'd failed. Failed the marriage. Failed Callie. Failed to give her what she wanted most, a family. It was done.

"Grant?" Chris, his stepdad, stood framed in the doorway, his eyes narrowed and his brows drawn together. "You okay?"

Grant hesitated, digging for his usual ability to play it cool, to mask his emotions. "I…"

"Come on in. It's just your mom and me tonight." Chris gently took his arm and pulled him into the kitchen where his mom was busy plating what looked like pork chops and red potatoes.

Her warm brown eyes lifted. The moment she saw his expression, she stepped away from the counter and wiped her hands on her cheerful striped apron. "Grant honey, what is it?"

He stood frozen to the spot, at a loss for words. She rushed around the granite island and enfolded him in her arms. She was a tall woman, lean and sturdy, and he felt like a boy again as she pulled him in close. His eyes squeezed shut and he hugged her back, the tension in his shoulders softening. Comfort from her genuine warmth and concern filled him.

When he stepped back, Chris handed him a chilled beer. "Have a seat and we'll discuss it over dinner."

Grant nodded and sank into a chair at the huge oak farm table where all family business and meals took place. "Where is everyone else?"

Sam and her husband, Holt, lived in one of the guesthouses and his other stepsister Amanda and her firefighter husband, Jake, lived in the other. Dylan and Gabriel lived in Solana Beach, but often dropped by for dinner.

His mom slid a plate loaded with two plump pork chops, a mountain of roasted potatoes, and spinach onto the woven green placemat in front of him. A fragrant aroma wafted up to his nostrils. "You kids don't all eat here every night. They've all got stuff going on. So you can just tell Chris and me what happened."

Not that he didn't love the rest of his family, but he appreciated not having a big audience. He took a long tug of the amber ale. Set it down, working to ignore the trembling in his hand. "The divorce is final. Just got the email and official documents from Callie." He dropped his head in his hands.

"Oh, Grant. Sweetie. I'm sorry." Angela stroked his hair, like she had when he'd been a little boy. "I know it hurts."

He shook his head and sat back. "That's the thing. It should hurt more. I just don't feel anything. Except that I couldn't make it work. That I don't have what it takes to make a marriage work."

Chris set down his beer. "Hey, that's not true. Do you hear me? Not true. It takes two people to make a marriage work or a marriage fail."

"Livvie said the same thing. But Callie sure seemed to think I wasn't there when it mattered. That my travel scheduled was to blame for her miscarrying and not being able to get pregnant again." Shit, now that he'd opened his mouth, he couldn't seem to stop.

He hadn't told anybody this. He'd even hidden most of it from Toby and Livvie until Mammoth. Until Livvie pushed him on it.

"Look at me," his mom demanded. "Olivia has always been wise beyond her years and she is absolutely right. When you and Callie met, she knew what your career entailed. She knew your passion was in traveling and photography when you married. Getting pregnant takes two and it is unfair for her to put that at your feet. I've known you your entire life and I am so proud of the man you are. A good man. A man who has carved out an incredible career, who has true friends, a family who loves him. Don't let the divorce mess with your head this way, okay?"

Grant swallowed and nodded. "I know all of that, but it still feels like I screwed up. That I don't have what it takes to do anything for the long-term."

"Bullshit." Chris smacked his hand on the sturdy wooden table. "Bullshit. Your relationship didn't work out and I'm sure you made mistakes and so did she. But you're human. That doesn't translate into you lacking character. You've always made me and your mom proud."

Angela's eyes shone with unshed tears. "Honey, you've been mourning since you came back last summer. That's natural. But don't let it color the rest of your life. You'll figure out what's next and I know you'll find a woman who appreciates you exactly as you are."

"Your mom and I found each other later in life and we were lucky to find love a second time. You'll find yours." Chris clasped his mom's hand and they smiled at each other.

Olivia's face popped up in his mind immediately. Time to switch the emotional episode off. "Thanks. I'll be fine. I'm starved. Let's eat." Grant picked up the fork and knife and cut into the juicy chop.

Out of his peripheral vision, he saw Chris and Angela exchange glances before they joined him.

A clean break was a good thing. Nowhere to move but forward. On his own.

Once the guard had waved her through the enormous wood and stone gate—after oohing and ahhing over her baby blue 1966 Mustang—Olivia relished the cruise up the curving road to the Pacific Vista Ranch stables. Rolling emerald hills adorned with lush clusters of towering trees, vibrant bougainvillea, and colorful flowers never failed to enchant her with their beauty. Her sense of awe that Grant actually got to live here hadn't diminished over the years.

Not that they hadn't grown up in a great neighborhood, but the ranch was like a secret magical oasis. Most of the estates in Rancho Santa Fe were veiled behind large gates, trees, and shrouded in privacy. The narrow winding roads through the community were lined with horse trails so people could ride without being concerned with avoiding traffic. Many people had no idea that a whole world of mini-ranches was tucked away just east of the sleepy beach towns of North County San Diego.

When she pulled up, Grant was leaning against the open doorway of the massive twenty-one stall stable where the McNeills housed their personal horses. Ironically, they called it the small stable because there were also four thirty-stall stables for the breeding business. Her stomach flip-flopped and she exhaled an unsteady breath––he looked ruggedly handsome in faded jeans and a navy and black flannel.

Determined to act natural, she squared her shoulders and stepped out into the sun-drenched day, welcoming the kiss of the feathery breeze and the warmth beaming down from the pristine blue sky. She strolled along the path toward him, gravel crunching beneath her boots, nerves dancing along her spine. A few muffled whinnies filled the air, but the early afternoon was otherwise tranquil. His amber eyes were concealed behind mirrored aviators, his lean face somber as he watched her approach.

She cleared her throat and waved one hand. "Hey." *Yeah, not awkward at all.*

He levered away from the doorframe, his mouth curving into a crooked half-smile. "Hey Livvie. Where's Toby?"

She shrugged one shoulder. "We were driving separately because he had some errands or something this morning."

Grant pulled his buzzing phone out of his pocket. "And he just texted." His brows drew together and his smile disappeared. "Shit."

She crossed the space separating them and his scent of laundry detergent and heated skin greeted her. She resisted the urge to sniff him. "Is he okay?"

Grant nodded, eyes glued to the screen. "Something came up today, but he can make the barbeque and wants to bring Erin."

Olivia tilted her head. "Wow, it's only been a week and he's having her meet your family?" Toby never moved fast in relationships.

Grant's eyebrows rose, his expression mirroring her surprise. "Right?"

Olivia paused to digest this new information. Now they

wouldn't have the buffer of Toby to help keep the dynamic on the friend level this afternoon. Not that it hadn't been awkward enough on the ride home from Mammoth. But she hadn't counted on being alone together yet. How could she act like nothing had changed?

Everything had changed. Simply standing a few feet away from him, a wave of longing whispered through her. Longing to wrap her arms around his broad shoulders and press her lips to the hollow at the base of his tanned throat. Longing to test whether their chemistry had been a fluke of being snowed in together.

Nope, she wasn't equipped to treat him like her best friend, at least not yet. Maybe riding would help.

"So, should we go anyway?" She forced a lighthearted note into her voice.

"Of course. Come on." Grant straightened and pivoted toward the barn's entrance. "I already saddled the horses. You're on Bonney. Let me text Jamie to see if he can take Sandy for a quick ride since Toby's not here."

"Oh, she's such a sweetheart. Do you think she'll remember me?" She grinned and followed him into the high-ceilinged building with stalls running along both sides.

Two gorgeous chestnuts, one with a white blaze, and a dark brown horse awaited them at the far end, where another open doorway led out to the sprawling expanse of the property. While Grant was on his phone, Olivia approached Bonney, the sweet twenty-year-old chestnut mare, and held out one hand. After a brief inspection, Bonney nuzzled her and Olivia gently stroked her face.

"Jamie's on his way, so let's go ahead and go." Grant swung up onto Major, all lean catlike grace.

She mounted and trotted out into the perfect San Diego day to where he waited. After a few minutes, she settled into the saddle and loosened the reins. Together they cantered out toward the open fields. The stress over feeling awkward dissipated as she settled into the joy of riding out in glorious nature.

"Are we staying on the ranch or going out onto the trails?" She actually didn't care one way or the other.

"Let's just hang on the ranch. I want to show you the pastures where some of the mares have already had their foals. You'll love it." Grant's jaw had softened.

"Awesome." Everything felt right all of a sudden. Maybe she'd overreacted earlier. Maybe they could be easy together. Friendly. Just like the decades of friendship pre-Mammoth-sexfest.

The next few hours flew by, alternating between meandering walking and bursts of exhilarating speed and even a brief stop at one of the pastures to admire some wobbly legged newborns who couldn't have been cuter.

Conversation was casual and ordinary––and smoothed out Olivia's nerves. They'd settled back into their familiar pattern. By the time they returned to the stables, she felt calmer and clearer than she had all week.

They dismounted and Jamie appeared before they had a chance to loosen the cinches. He shooed them away, insisting on removing the tack, claiming both horses needed grooming.

"You brought a change of clothes, right? Let's go to my place and we can clean up. We've got about an hour before they expect us up at the main house," Grant said.

Olivia nibbled on the inside of her cheek. It was one thing when the three of them were all going to change and have a pre-dinner drink at Grant's. Now it would be the two of them.

Changing clothes. Which meant a period of time with no clothes. Naked and alone. In the same house. Just like last weekend. The hairs on the nape of her neck prickled and her pulse quickened.

She cleared her throat. "I did. Do you want to ride over with me?" The guesthouse was a short walk, but she'd rather have her car so she could leave straight after dinner.

Now Grant hesitated, then nodded. "Yeah, let's go."

They climbed into her vintage Mustang and she turned the key in the ignition. It purred to a start, smooth and sexy.

He smoothed his hand along the dashboard and turned to her, his lips curving up. "You weren't kidding that she's in better condition now than she was in high school. This car holds some great memories."

She beamed. "Well, the stereo is now state of the art--as much as possible for an antique. I went stealth with a stereo receiver in the glove box so I can use Bluetooth and all my music. There's a pair of speakers in the back with an amp and subwoofer so the sound is way better than it was back in the day."

He stared at her, eyes wide, and then he chuckled. "Livvie, you are one of a kind. And I love that you found an antique radio to make it look like the original."

She rolled her eyes, then gazed over her shoulder to back up. "Right? And I've never claimed to be anyone other than a major nerd. As are you. And I think we had some of our deepest discussions in this car."

He threw up his hands. "Guilty. Discussions on what we were going to do with our lives. And I think my favorite times were when the three of us parked and listened to music. It all seemed so important then."

She navigated up the drive toward the second guesthouse, Grant's current home. She parked. "My favorite night was one when it was just you and me. Not sure what Toby was doing. We were parked outside of my old house until the sun came up and I brought you over to my way of thinking about the genius of The Cure. Remember?"

"Hell yeah. You made me listen to those albums for hours, determined to convince me they weren't just depressing dudes with an eyeliner fetish."

"And I was right, wasn't I? I knew if you heard the right songs--not just the ones that got all the radio play--you'd fall for them too. How many times did I play 'Boys Don't Cry'?"

"I don't know. Fifty? Sixty times? You were determined to memorize it and you kept messing up on the third verse." He was laughing hard now, rocking forward in his seat.

"And I'd rewind the CD and start from the beginning. Over and over and over again. Oh my god. To be seventeen again." To this day, she couldn't listen to that song without thinking of Grant. Especially the line, "just keep on laughing, hiding the tears in my eyes." Grant was the master of disguising his feelings.

"I couldn't get that song out of my head for weeks." He shook his head. "And anytime I hear The Cure, it reminds me of you."

"Me too." She angled toward him and before she could consider the consequences, she stroked his muscular forearm.

He sucked in a breath, yanked open the door, and bolted out. "Okay, let's go in."

She squeezed her eyes shut for a moment. Of course, touching him immediately triggered sparks between them-- foolish move on her part. Even though she'd been playing with the idea of them hooking up again before she left. A secret fling until she jetted off to Crete. Apparently, he had not.

She took her time exiting the car and grabbed her duffle bag from the back seat. Grant was already in the house, leaving the front door ajar. Irritating. She glanced at her watch––could they make it through forty-five minutes safely until they'd join his family?

She followed the clanking of dishes. The marble-tiled hallway opened up to the chef's kitchen and vast great room, with high wood-beamed ceilings, large stone fireplace, and gleaming windows. Grant stood behind the pale gray granite island, pouring blond ale into a couple pint glasses.

He glanced up from his task but didn't quite meet her gaze. "You can use the first guest room. The bathroom should be stocked."

She rested her hands against one of the barstools, gripping the navy upholstery. "Grant."

He looked up, his eyes wary, his jaw tight. "We should get moving. You know my mom doesn't like anyone coming in late."

"Look, I know we're pretending in front of everyone else that last weekend never happened, but I don't deserve the signature Michaels freeze." Anger and hurt tangled in her heart.

"I'm not trying to freeze you out. It's just when you touch me, I..." He winced and scrubbed his hands through his windswept hair.

Her fingers dug into the seat back. "Well, if you won't look at me when we're up at the house, people will notice. I thought you were the one who was the expert at hiding feelings."

He slapped his hands on the counter. "Damn it, Livvie. What do you want me to say? I'm doing the best I can, but seeing you is hard."

She stiffened. "It's hard for me too. So you're throwing in the towel?"

He pivoted and stalked away toward the two large L-shaped charcoal gray couches and flung himself down on one, dropping his head in his hands. When he didn't speak, she walked over and perched on the edge of the other sofa. Waited.

He lifted his head, his golden eyes intense, his brows drawn together. "No. I don't know. Damn it. I don't know what the hell to do."

Her breath whooshed out and her flare of anger subsided. Okay, not so cold after all. "I don't know either. But we promised we would remain friends and we've always been honest with each other. Your mom and Toby and everyone will know something is up if we tiptoe around each other. We need a plan."

He massaged the back of his neck and considered her. "A plan?"

"Yeah. You and Toby are my best friends and I want to spend time with you before I leave in two months. So we need to find a way to be friends because I can't lose you." She crossed her legs and smoothed her now damp palms along her jeans. Her pulse hammered a staccato beat in her temples.

"Agreed. I don't know about a plan, but we need to act casual tonight."

Disappointment coursed through her, even though she didn't have any answers either. Why had she expected him to react differently? To either sweep her up into his arms and carry her off to his bedroom or offer some words of wisdom. She'd witnessed his impassive, cool demeanor directed toward others over the years, but had never been the recipient.

She didn't care for it one bit.

She clasped her hands in her lap. On one hand she knew they needed to "act casual" and not let anyone in on their explosive secret. But on the other, she wanted him to *do* something. Yes, she didn't want to lose him as her best friend, but last weekend had given her a glimpse into what they'd be like as a couple and it was beyond her wildest romantic imaginings. Her best friend and the best sex she'd ever had. Maybe the intensity was because of the circumstances.

Now that she'd seen him again, her heart was indicating to her that was not the case. She had fallen in love with him and nothing was the same.

Everything was wrong. Why had this happened two months before she was embarking on the opportunity of a lifetime? Maybe if she weren't going to Greece, they could give their changed relationship a chance? Or hell, even try long distance--she planned to return to San Diego in a year. Did she remain silent now and pursue it next March?

Judging from his reaction today, he didn't share her feelings. He wanted to forget, not explore. Which was more practical and smart. But she was tired of always being practical, smart Olivia. Tired of being responsible and reliable and realistic.

She'd promised him she could handle them hooking up but hadn't realized how tough it would actually be.

She couldn't destroy their friendship. He needed her to be his friend, especially now he was at a major crossroads in his life--getting divorced, trying to figure out the new path for his career, starting over essentially in every area. They'd always been each other's rocks through thick and thin.

She couldn't imagine her life without him and Toby. And if she revealed her newly discovered feelings to Grant when he was bolting back into the friend zone, it could impact all their friendships. And if Toby found out they'd lied to him, he'd feel awkward at best, betrayed at worst. The Three Musketeers had endured almost two decades. No way could she be the one responsible for destroying the one true thing Grant had to rely on right now.

. . .

SHE ROSE FROM THE COUCH. "Got it. Casual. Buddies. I'm sure I can act as cool and composed as you if I try. I'm going to shower. Meet you out here in thirty." She marched to the first bedroom, snatching up her weekend tote bag.

"Livvie," he called, his voice strained.

She waved one hand and didn't stop until she'd closed the bedroom door behind her. Time to flip on autopilot, get ready, and tuck her emotions away. She could compartmentalize too.

But she'd look good doing it. She'd brought her favorite jeans and one of her favorite tops--an incredibly flattering sapphire blue that enhanced her eyes and made her boobs look like more than the small handfuls they were.

Sure, she was being perverse because wanting Grant to drool over her wasn't exactly the most expeditious path toward getting their friendship back on even footing. But right now, her heart hurt, her head was confused, and conse-quences be damned.

CHAPTER 18

Grant strummed his fingers on his denim-clad thigh and fought to focus his gaze straight through the windshield and not side-eye Olivia. Especially after he'd been the one emphasizing that they needed to make sure nobody suspected the new element to their relationship. But damn, she'd strolled out with her hair flowing around her creamy shoulders and that red lipstick that had been his undoing every time she wore it. He needed to face the fact that he'd probably never see her as his buddy/sister/friend again without wanting more.

But she deserved to have a chance at finding love with someone who was worthy of her, not her freshly divorced best friend who basically had no career plan. She needed him as her support system and friend, like he'd always been. What they'd always been to each other. It would just take a little more time, that was all. It hadn't even been a full week since he'd been buried inside her, with her long, toned legs wrapped around him.

He shifted in his seat, adjusting his pants and willing his dick to remain silent. The pristine backseat didn't give him any ideas either. *Right.* Thankfully, it was a one-minute drive to the main house. He almost cried in relief when she parked and he never cried. He bolted out and circled around the back of the car to wait for her.

Before they could reach the gigantic wooden front door, Toby swung his SUV into the parking spot next to Livvie's Mustang and called out, "Hey guys, wait up and we'll come in with you."

Toby and Erin exited the truck and joined them.

"Wow. This place is incredible. You grew up here?" Erin's eyes bugged as she checked out the estate and the surrounding clusters of trees and vividly colored flower beds framing the front entrance.

Grant knew that feeling. When he and his brothers had moved to Pacific Vista Ranch as teenagers, they'd been fish out of water. Even now, years later, Grant never took for granted the sprawling Spanish-style cream-colored home with its terracotta tiled roof, enormous windows, and endless acres of natural beauty. Now it was simply home.

"I moved here in high school. Now I live in one of the guesthouses down the way." He waved a hand toward the stables and other buildings farther down the drive.

"Lucky you," Erin said. "Thanks so much for allowing me to join you."

"Wouldn't have come without you, babe." Toby slid his arm around Erin, who nestled in next to him, turning her face upward. He lowered his head and kissed her.

Livvie goggled, her eyebrows disappearing beneath her bangs before she caught Grant's gaze. Toby was never one for PDA.

Toby lifted his head and chuckled. "Stop staring. We like each other, okay? We're still the Three Musketeers even if I've got a girlfriend now."

A girlfriend? After a week? Livvie recovered first. "Not staring. Just not used to seeing you with a better half."

"You got the better half right. I dunno, there was something magic about Mammoth. Didn't get to hold my event, but spending time snowed in with Erin made it worth it." He gazed down at her, a goofy grin plastered to his face.

Grant jolted. Damn right there was something about Mammoth——it sure as hell had transformed his and Livvie's relationship. He ran his tongue around his teeth before responding. "Don't mind us, Erin. Toby doesn't usually bring girls around."

She beamed and leaned her head against Toby's shoulder. "That's what I like to hear. He's special. And I hope you two aren't mad at me for keeping him all to myself during the snowstorm."

"Oh, don't worry about it——it gave Grant and me time to catch up." Olivia flashed her straight white teeth and studiously avoided looking at him.

Grant stuffed his hands in his pockets and nodded. Suddenly a fur-covered rocket galloped up to them, bumping against his legs. Saved by the dog.

"Stella. Hey, good girl." Grant crouched down and scrubbed his hands over the golden-brown mutt's joyous face.

Olivia reached down and scratched between the dog's ears and her hair swung forward, the fresh fruity scent making his mouth water. Drooling over her, just like the dog.

"Hey, you guys coming in? We've got rolled tacos and they will be gone if you don't get in here ASAP," Samantha McNeill Ericsson, Grant's stepsister, bellowed from the front door.

Grant blew out a huge breath, grateful for the distraction. Sam was a petite redhead notorious for her appetite. She could eat more than any of the ranch hands, so her threat about the tacos wasn't an idle one.

"Sam, it's been too long." Olivia rushed over and hugged her.

Sam grinned and hooked her arm through Olivia's. "You're always welcome here. You and Toby are family."

Grant winced at the reminder. Olivia was *family*. Olivia was his *best friend*. Olivia was most definitely *not his girlfriend*. He'd do well to keep that unequivocal fact front and center of his mind.

And if he needed to avoid her in an unobtrusive way tonight, so be it. They had time to get back into the friend zone, even though it felt impossible right now. Time to enjoy the early evening barbeque with his family and friends.

Sam and Olivia led the way into the broad hallway with its high ceilings and pale walls dotted with richly colored paintings. Stella loped along beside them, her tail wagging like a metronome--oh to have her simple happy life. Grant chatted with Toby and Erin and stared at everything but Olivia's very fine ass.

Voices floated from the arched doorway leading into the massive great room and open kitchen. When they entered the spacious area, mouthwatering scents filled the room, and his stomach rumbled. Platters of hors d'œuvres were spread along the granite island, along with a jumbo pitcher of classic margaritas.

His mom peeked up from filling a huge clear bowl with blue corn tortilla chips. Round dishes of guacamole and three kinds of salsa were waiting to be sampled. Their family preferred it spicy, but they'd had a few incidents where guests had steam pumping from their ears and they'd learned to offer the mildest salsa too.

Grant strode to his mom and enveloped her in a one-arm

hug, pressed a kiss on her cheek, and snaked a handful of chips with the other.

She squeezed him and her deep brown eyes searched his face, a wrinkle of worry between her brows. "You okay, sweetie?"

"Yeah. I'm starving." He retreated, angled toward the counter, and scooped up a dollop of guac. Took a bite and groaned. "Your guac even beats Fidel's."

"Okay, I'll take the hint. You always give me outlandish compliments when you don't want to talk." Her lips twitched. "Where are your friends?"

"Livvie's over with the twins and Toby brought a girl." Grant waved Toby and Erin over. Sighed an internal sigh of relief that Livvie was huddled up with Sam and Dylan. They'd always gotten along so well--his family adored her.

Angela greeted Toby and Erin with a welcoming smile. "So nice to see you, Toby. I was sorry to hear that your expo was canceled because of the blizzard."

He still had Erin plastered to his side. "Silver linings, Mrs. M. If we'd had the event, I wouldn't have been able to spend so much time alone with this gorgeous woman. This is Erin." His eyes glowed and his grin was wide.

Chris joined them at the counter and patted Grant's shoulder. "Nice to see you, Toby and Erin. I'm Chris McNeill.

"That's so sweet. Erin, it's lovely to meet you. Can I pour you both a margarita?" Angela asked. When they both nodded, she filled two glasses for them.

"So, the four of you were snowed in together? Grant didn't share much about the weekend with us," Chris said.

"Oh, it wasn't the four of us. Toby stayed with me." Erin's lips curved up, completely unaware that she'd just spilled a secret.

Grant's molars ground together. Shit. He hadn't

mentioned that he and Livvie had been alone the majority of the weekend. Not that he was trying to hide it or that anyone would think twice, but his mom never missed a detail.

Angela laid a hand on her chest and turned toward him. "I didn't realize that. I assumed you were all together."

Grant ignored the heat of her gaze and studiously dug into the guacamole. "Nope."

"Olivia, come say hi." His mom waved her over. *Crap.*

Olivia smiled and strolled over. "Hi, Angela. Hi, Chris. It's great to see you both."

"You look wonderful, honey. We hope to see more of you and Toby now that Grant's back for good," Angela said.

Olivia lowered her lashes, then her lips curved up. "It's definitely been too long. And it's great everyone is here. Dylan mentioned that Ryan is moving back. What about Austin?"

Grant's shoulders relaxed. "Yeah, Ryan should be here soon and Austin later this year." Olivia didn't know the topic of discussion before she'd come over, but she was doing an excellent job of steering it in a new direction.

Angela leaned back against Chris. "All my boys back in San Diego. It's a dream come true."

"How's everything down at the library, Olivia?" Chris asked.

"It's great. And actually I have some news. I've accepted a year-long position in Greece curating a couple special collections and will be leaving in a couple of months."

Grant's gut tightened, but he tamped it down. Olivia deserved to live her life fully and circumstances had prevented her freedom for too long. And hadn't he figured the distance would be the antidote to get him thinking about her as his platonic friend again? It was perfect.

Hell, it should have been perfect.

"What timing. Grant finally comes home and you're leaving. That's too bad. But I'm so happy for you. I know how much you've wanted to travel," Angela said.

"It's an amazing opportunity. Now that my mom is doing well and my aunt Rose lives with her, I finally feel okay going." Livvie's face lit up, her blue eyes sparkling.

"You deserve everything wonderful that comes your way. Hold on, I'm going to pop a bottle of bubbly for a toast. It's just incredible news." Chris turned to the refrigerator and pulled out a bottle of Veuve.

"Hey everyone, come on over, we're toasting Olivia moving to Greece for a year," Angela called while rifling through the cabinet for champagne flutes.

Sam, Dylan, and Amanda and their husbands Holt, Gabriel, and Jake joined them around the large island. Holt had been a top Hollywood stuntman for years before retiring and starting his own agency. Gabriel was a French soccer celebrity whose career had come to an abrupt end when he blew out his knee. Now he was a part-time commentator and spent part of his time cultivating vines for a future wine business, like the one his family ran in France. Jake was a firefighter who had crushed on Amanda in high school and reconnected with her when he'd sought her help after rescuing Stella from a hit-and-run accident.

His stepsisters were all now happily married and he liked all the guys. The couples epitomized how marriage could be when a person met their match. And suddenly Grant realized he envied them a bit.

Jake's brother Rafael Cruz and his fiancée, Phoebe, joined them. They were both witty, scary smart, and senior partners at a wealth management firm in La Jolla.

When had everyone gotten paired up? Granted, they were in their thirties now, so it was the time for marriage, kids, and all that business.

He'd screwed up his chance.

He rubbed the tight bands of muscle on the back of his neck, willing the tension to dissipate. The strain of seeing Olivia and recognizing he couldn't simply tuck away their weekend in the vault. The fear they may have ruined their decades-old friendship.

And now Toby had seemingly fallen in love overnight and couldn't keep his eyes and hands off his new girlfriend. What were the odds? But introducing an outside person was different than two of the Three Musketeers hooking up and changing the three-friends dynamic. Wasn't it?

"Grant." His mom handed him a glass of champagne, her eyes speculative again.

Everyone was staring. Everyone except Livvie. He raised his arm and forced a smile. "Sorry. Here's to Livvie going to Greece."

They toasted and tossed back the bubbly.

"Load up with snacks, everyone. Chris won't be firing up the grill for a little while." Angela waved her hands to the spread. "Then we'll move back by the pool."

The conversations buzzed around them. Grant needed a beer. He looked up to find Olivia staring at him, her ocean eyes quizzical. Damn, she could always read his moods.

"Want a beer?" he asked.

She nodded and circled around the island to join him. "Sure."

He snagged two from the stainless steel, double-door refrigerator, twisted off the lids, and handed her one chilled bottle. Their fingers brushed, sparks shooting up his arm from the brief contact. He leaned against the counter and studied her. "So how about Toby?"

She peeked over her shoulder to make sure Toby wasn't within earshot and waved a hand in the air. "Can you believe it? I never thought I'd see the day he'd be a total goner. I love it."

His lips twitched. "Goner is right. He's got little arrows and hearts floating over his head. I just hope she's as cool as she seems."

"Okay, cynical one. She seems nice and really into him." Her dark brows drew together.

"For now." He shrugged. Callie had been really nice and into him. Until she wasn't.

Her lips thinned. "Come on. Don't be like that. And it takes two. Maybe he'll fall out as fast as he fell in. You know, switch it on and off."

He stiffened. Was she referring to him now? He paused and drank more beer.

Before he could respond, Angela returned. "Well, I think it's pretty clear what those two were doing while snowed in, but what about you two? You didn't mention that."

A pink flush stained Olivia's high cheekbones and she cleared her throat before speaking quickly. "It was just for a day. We got to catch up on the last few years in person instead of FaceTime. Grant took some photos and we built a snowman, just like when you'd take us up to the mountains when we were kids."

"Yeah, and the place we stayed was killer, with a fireplace and Jacuzzi. I made my carbonara. We played some games, you know." A nerve twitched behind his eye, hating being anything less than honest with his mom.

Angela smiled and looked between them. "I think it's wonderful. You two have always had such a special bond, so it must have been nice to spend some time reconnecting."

"Yeah, reconnecting." Olivia nodded her head vigorously.

"Definitely great. Anything you need me to do, Mom?" If they stood here any longer chatting, his mom would sense something was up. She was one of the few people who could read him and right now her Spidey sense was tingling.

"No, you just enjoy yourself with Olivia. Especially now

we know she's leaving. I'm going to check in with Sam to make sure she didn't polish off all the tacos."

Despite the noise from lively chatter, shouts of laughter, and the hum of bluesy background music, it seemed all he could focus on was Livvie. Why was everything suddenly so damn complicated? They sipped their beers in silence and she appeared as lost in her own thoughts as he was.

"What's up with you guys? Everything okay?" Toby and Erin, attached at the hip, joined them in the kitchen.

Olivia straightened with a slight shake of her head. "Nothing. Everything's fine."

"Yeah, all cool here." *Play it cool in front of Toby.*

"Erin and I were just talking about how cool Greece sounds and how maybe we could all go visit Livvie in the summer. What do you think?" Toby asked.

Grant could only stare. When he glanced at Olivia, her jaw had dropped. They were already talking about going to Europe together after one week? Had an alien come down and taken over his perpetually single buddy's body or what?

"Umm...sure. I mean, we already talked about you guys coming over at some point, right?" Olivia asked. Her smile was strained.

Grant cleared his throat. "Things are up in the air for me right now. It will all depend on what I end up doing for work."

Olivia whipped her head toward him. "We decided you guys were coming, right?" Hurt shone in her eyes.

"Yeah, man, of course we'll make the timing work. And you'll be itching to travel by then. Right?" Toby's broad grin dimmed for the first time today.

Grant shrugged one shoulder. "I don't want to hold anyone back. And I'm already feeling the urge to take off. But I want to see if I can make things work from San Diego."

Toby looked down at Erin. "Grant's always been a road

warrior and he just moved back from Australia last summer. He makes my travel schedule look tame."

And Grant was over the conversation. Flitting off to Greece wouldn't exactly align with his goal of being stable and grounded in one place. The last thing he wanted to dive into now was why he'd left Australia, which led to his failed marriage, and a host of other shit he wasn't going to discuss tonight.

Olivia, always the diplomat, stepped closer and rubbed his shoulder. "It will all work out. I know it."

"Time to move this party outside. Everybody grab something and carry it to the patio, please," Sam called out.

Grant gave her a thumbs up, grateful for the interruption. Saved by the barbeque.

One step closer to this day ending and him being able to retreat to his house and brood in peace. Alone.

CHAPTER 19

"Crap." Olivia smacked the rear quarter panel of her beloved car, glared up at the black sky, and cursed the lack of streetlamps. Most of the Rancho Santa Fe estates were set far back from the road and shrouded with hedges or trees, so even though it wasn't late, it felt like the middle of the night. Usually, she appreciated the dazzling clusters of stars visible out here, but they weren't doing her any favors this evening.

With her gas tank empty and her Mustang marooned on the sorry sliver of gravel which served as a shoulder, the lack of artificial light was a major hindrance. The flashing of her hazards didn't help and their loud clicking grated on her already frayed nerves.

Of course, she didn't have a roadside service plan because she could take care of any mechanical issues by herself, thank you very much. An empty gas tank, however, served up a different type of dilemma. She couldn't very well fuel the car herself.

She was several miles from the nearest gas station and

while a great deal of the roads had horse trails she could safely traverse, many didn't. The winding roads were narrow and she'd be foolish to try to walk far in the darkness.

She'd only made it two miles or so from the ranch when her car sputtered and died. There were many benefits to having a vintage beauty of a car, but her gas gauge had stopped working last month and she'd forgotten to fix it. She knew roughly how far she could travel on a tank of gas, but this week she'd been preoccupied. Absentminded. Her usual strict attention to detail nowhere to be found.

Grant Michaels on the brain.

And so here she sat. Because today hadn't been challenging enough. She snorted and shoved her bangs off her forehead.

When she'd finally made her excuses to leave, her whole body had sagged in relief. She'd switched to drinking water hours ago, knowing she would need to cut out early. The stress of pretending with Grant, and everyone else for that matter, had taken its toll. Toby had seemed oblivious––thank you, Erin––but only because he was riding an infatuation buzz.

Sadly, her infatuation high wasn't one to celebrate, but more like an infatuation disaster. She'd even considered propositioning Grant before she'd first arrived this afternoon. The week had been tough pining over him, and she was leaving in March.

Both of them knew the distance would help them return to the friendship balance, so why not see each other until then? That way they could truly enjoy each other and remove the awkwardness between them, at least when they were alone. And how naïve was she?

Her plan had wobbled the minute she saw him at the stables and then poofed into thin air once they were at his house. She rubbed her chest, her heart aching. And now she needed him to rescue her from her own absentmindedness. Damn it.

She would have preferred to call Toby, but he and Erin had left before she had and were likely already in bed. Aunt Rose wasn't familiar with the roads in Rancho Santa Fe and would probably run her over. Not an option. Grant always came through for her, from the time in junior high when he'd told off the pack of bullies teasing her about her "four-eyes" to talking to her on the phone late into the night when she'd been struggling to care for her mom.

She slid back into the front seat and drummed her fingers on the leather steering wheel. Of course, not a single car had passed by. Not that she would get in a car with a stranger anyways. She thunked her head against the headrest and groaned. How could she have been so careless?

But she couldn't sit here all night, so she fished her phone out of her satchel and tapped Grant's number, which of course was number one on her list of favorites. The phone rang and rang until his voicemail clicked on. Great.

She left a message, with her vague whereabouts––ten steps past such-and-such street, and around the corner from that really big tree and almost to that hairpin curve in the road. Then she texted him a SOS and hoped for the best.

Her phone pinged. *Usual route home??*

Yes. No, I decided to take the scenic route, what do you think? No need for her to be snarky toward him when he was saving her ass.

Be there in 10. Sit tight and make sure hazards are on.

She rolled her eyes and replied with a thumbs-up. Seriously? Did he really think she'd just sit there in the dark waiting for someone to hit her? Geez.

You never knew though. She exited the car again and

moved to the shoulder. Just in case some reckless driver came careening around the hairpin turn behind her. A loud crack sounded in the line of trees behind her and she jumped. A few rustles and crunches punctuated the silence.

She shivered, smoothed her hair away from her face, and turned so her back was to her car. There were coyotes all over the place, but it was probably just a deer or a rabbit. A sweet little bunny, not a hungry predator with sharp pointy teeth. She flipped her phone's flashlight and scanned the thick shrubbery. Just in case some furry creature wanted to venture out to say hello.

Or bite a chunk off her thigh.

Before her imagination could run too wild, one of her favorite sounds greeted her ears, the purr of an engine, followed by the illumination from a pair of headlights pulling up behind her. Grant's battered charcoal gray jeep. She released a deep breath, pushed away from the car, and strode to the passenger door.

She climbed inside and slammed the door behind her. "Thanks for coming."

"No problem. You lock the doors?" He gestured toward her Mustang.

"I did. You have a gas can?" She turned in the seat to look at him. She couldn't read his expression in the dim light.

He grunted his assent and pulled around her car, heading toward El Camino Real, the closest gas station.

They rode in silence for a few minutes as he expertly navigated the twists and turns. Was he giving her the silent treatment? They hadn't spoken much over the last few hours of the barbeque although she hadn't taken her gaze off him for a moment. The strain around his eyes and grooves around his mouth had signaled his unhappiness to anyone who knew him well.

She sighed. "Look, I already feel like an idiot for gambling on my gas gauge and losing. Thank you for coming to the rescue."

The corner of his mouth quirked up. "I wouldn't call it rescuing. Just helping out a friend."

She pounced. "So you're my friend again? After today, I wasn't so sure." His "casual" act all evening hurt.

He threaded one hand through his hair and sighed. "Don't do this."

"Don't do what? You say you don't want to lose our friendship, but you avoided me all night." She angled in the seat to face him.

He winced. "We agreed we needed to act like nothing had changed. And I'm here right now, aren't I?"

She harrumphed. "Well of course you are. You're always here for me when I need you. But that's more because you're a solid, responsible guy. You'd do it for anyone."

He shook his head. "Yeah, that's my reputation. Responsible."

Her brows drew together. *Something more here.* "Yes. Responsible. There for the people you care about. There for every company you've worked for in your life. What's this about? Tell me what's going on."

He pulled onto Encinitas Boulevard and she caught the tightness in his jaw, the iron grip on the steering wheel when he slowed for the red light. His eyes closed for a moment and he angled toward her, and pain shone through his golden eyes.

"It's kind of awkward now that we..." He blew out a breath. "The final divorce decree came this week. Hit me with the reality of it all. Callie always called me irresponsible. Flaky."

Outrage stiffened her spine. "What? You are not flaky or irresponsible. How dare she?"

The light turned green and Grant hit the gas. "Look, we

were married. She saw sides of me nobody else has. I wasn't there when she miscarried. I was gone a lot."

"I've known you since you were twelve years old, so I'd say I've seen all sides of you. When you guys married, she knew about your career, right?"

He nodded.

"Was it an issue then? Was she confused? Did she think you'd all of a sudden be around all the time?" Righteous anger filled her system.

"Well, no. But when she was pregnant, she asked me to not travel so much. And I basically blew her off because I got some really great gigs."

"And it was somehow you fault because you weren't there." Olivia's heart ached for him. For them. But... She reached across and squeezed his leg. "You know it wasn't your fault, right?

The giant gas station sign illuminated the car with a sudden burst of neon light as Grant pulled into the pump. He shifted the car into park and turned to her. "No, I don't know that. Maybe if she weren't so angry with me all the time, it would have been different. Let me get the gas."

He jumped out, popped the back hatch, and pulled out an empty red plastic gasoline container. He strode to the pump, keeping his back to her. His broad shoulders were stiff, his gaze fixed on the nozzle and fuel.

Olivia sat in the car, leaned her head back against the headrest, and closed her eyes. Poor Grant did believe his divorce was all his fault. Didn't he realize if he were truly irresponsible, that would never occur to him? If he were some flaky nomad always seeking the next adventure, he simply wouldn't care. Another flicker of anger at Callie went through her, but she fought to be sympathetic. As a couple, the two of them had gone through a tragic nightmare. But to blame it all on Grant wasn't fair. It took two.

When he was finished, he climbed in and turned to her. "I don't want to talk about it, okay?"

She nodded. "Sure. But can I say something?"

He turned on the engine and eased out of the gas station. "I don't want to talk about it. Okay?" he repeated, his jaw rigid, his gaze straight ahead.

"You don't have to talk. Just listen. I want to remind you of a few things. You are the type of person people rely on. That's not conditional on always being in one place. No matter where you traveled, you always made time to talk to me or respond to my emails. No matter what." She blinked back the moisture gathering in her eyes.

Damn it, she wouldn't cry over this, but he needed to understand. "You have been the best friend to me and to Toby. And you have always been there for your mom. For your family. You excelled at every single job you've done. That is *not* the track record of a flake."

He reached out a hand and clasped hers. "Livvie. You're biased. You make me sound like a fucking saint. And I'm not."

She growled. "Oh please. I wouldn't be your friend if you were a fucking saint. Who wants to be with a saint? You're human. You make mistakes. We all do. I don't know what kind of standard you're trying to hold yourself to, but stop it. Just stop it." She smacked the dashboard.

His mouth dropped open. "You're yelling at me, Olivia Hanlon. You never raise your voice."

"I can yell if I want. Who says librarians can't yell? You're just being stubborn and, frankly, being a martyr."

"A martyr? You've got to be kidding me." His voice rose a few octaves.

"Now who is shouting? Yes, a martyr. You aren't the first person in this world to get divorced. You aren't the first person in the world to screw up a relationship. I mean, do you think I'm a flake? I haven't even gotten close to marriage and I'm thirty-three years old. At least you tried. You were brave enough to try." She turned all the way in her seat, her hands flying up to emphasize her point.

He cut the engine and Olivia looked around. They were back at her car already.

"Look, I don't want to fight with you. I'm not a martyr. I'm just a mess. I've got to get my life together." His voice was resigned. Quiet.

"Yes, you do. And you are on track to do that. You've had an incredibly successful career. You just need to figure out the next step. That's all. And I'm sorry, but I know you better than anyone and I will not allow you to continue blaming yourself for everything. Got it?"

He chuckled. "What would I do without you?"

She gave him a light punch on the arm. "You'd be one miserable bastard, that's what."

He shook his head, then straightened. "You're right. But I am wiped. Let's get your gas tank handled so we can call it a night."

Regret snaked through her. At least she'd been able to lighten his mood a little bit. She'd always been able to coax him out of his melancholy and at least glimpse the bright side. Tonight, she'd be his best friend and help him through a tough patch. Just as he helped her out of a scrape. Because that was what best friends did.

Even though she'd love to invite him over, she couldn't ignore the fatigue and worry all over him. She could bury the feelings that had become undeniable since they'd returned from Mammoth. For tonight, anyway. The absolute knowledge that she loved him in every way, not just the way she'd accepted since she they had met.

Because she couldn't be happy until she had a taste of freedom. Experienced new cultures, savored new cuisine, explored everything out there beyond San Diego. Nothing could stop her from going to Greece. From traveling the world.

Grant needed time to figure out that he was responsible and could be rooted in one place.

But her heart ached.

CHAPTER 20

*G*rant slugged down half a bottle of water, leaned against the split-rail fence, and admired the mares grazing in the verdant pasture. The January sunshine was unseasonably warm again today and his flannel shirt stuck to the skin between his shoulder blades. Working for his stepsister was fulfilling, exhausting, and an excellent way to experience living in one place for several months. And he looked forward to his brothers Ryan and Austin moving back to San Diego.

Although he loved spending time with his family and living in the guesthouse, this transition period was coming to a close for him. He couldn't ignore the restlessness simmering in his blood much longer. He missed being behind his camera capturing exhilarating sports or unusual locations. From shooting big wave surfers off the coast of Biarritz, France, to ancient monuments in Italy, to the Winter Olympics, to capturing shots of the Great Barrier Reef in Australia, he fed off the excitement. It filled him in a way nothing else could.

Except for time spent with Livvie. But he'd been trying to

keep his distance this week, because seeing her was tougher than he'd anticipated. His feelings were anything but platonic for her anymore. But he wouldn't be selfish like he'd been in his marriage, not again.

Even if Livvie had fallen for him too, she had her own dreams, dreams that didn't include staying in San Diego with him. He cared about her too deeply to throw a wrench in her plans or give her cause to hesitate. Maybe circumstances would change and in a year everything would look different.

His phone buzzed and he pulled it out of his back pocket. An unfamiliar number from a Los Angeles area code. When he answered, a man's smooth voice asked, "Can I speak to Grant Michaels?"

"You're speaking to him."

"This is Matt King. You reached out a few months ago about shooting some of our surf competitions in Huntington Beach and Oceanside? You still up for freelance gigs?"

Grant's heart rate kicked up. "Yes, I did. My buddy Joe Louis referred me to you. We've worked on a lot of——"

"I know your work——you're one of the best. This is kind of last-minute, but I've got a surf exhibition this weekend in Huntington and need another photographer. You up for it?" Matt's voice was brusque. Matter-of-fact.

Grant shoved away from the fence and paced around the gravel path, a grin breaking across his face. "Absolutely. Tell me when and where and I'm there."

"South Side of the HB Pier. You'll see the vans. The breaks are pretty distant this time of year, so take that into account with your gear. 5:45 a.m. too early?"

Grant paused and savored the moment. "Nope. And is this a one-off or are you looking for the season?"

"I'm looking for someone to add to the regular freelance roster. If all goes well this weekend, you can choose to take as many or as few as you want. Travel is covered and we'll be hitting Portugal, France, and Australia, to name a few spots."

Grant pumped one fist in the air. "That's perfect. I'm not planning on as much travel as I've done in the past, but a few trips a year would be great."

"Awesome. Save my number and I'll see you Saturday. Thanks, bro." Matt hung up.

He slid his phone back into his pocket and pumped both fists in the air. "Yes."

"Talking to the mares now?" Sam approached from the breeding barn, her boots crunching along the packed ground, her dark eyes dancing with laughter.

He chuckled, the weight around his shoulders lightening a bit. "Like you don't talk to the horses every day?"

She laughed. "Busted. And they answer me." She tilted her head, her thick auburn braid swinging over her shoulder, and studied him. "What's got you looking so giddy?"

"Giddy?" He wrinkled his nose. "Please. Actually, some great news. A shoot up in Huntington Beach Saturday morning––surfing expo."

She clasped both of his hands and squeezed. "That's great. And I was wondering when you'd finally get around to work again."

"Hey, smartass. I work my ass off here." His lips twitched.

She winked and her smile faded. "You've been doing a great job and I love having you back at the ranch. But you're a photographer. And you haven't been happy. Not really."

"I––"

She shook her head. "Don't. I know you. And you've beaten yourself up long enough. Angela told me the divorce is finally official, but you two were done for years. Time to move on."

Sam was blunt and accurate, as usual. He and Callie had been finished months before their formal separation. But the fact they'd been miserable didn't help him feel less like an asshole. "Yeah, I know. I just--"

Sam held up her hands. "Just nothing. What you need is to focus on finding the right balance of travel and home, that's all. Some of us, like me, are truly tethered to one spot. The ranch is my place. Dylan never belonged here the same way and she's my twin. You'll figure it out. And you'll fall in love again."

He stiffened. He'd already fallen in love. With his best friend. And she was leaving the country. "I'll find it." He managed a shrug.

"That's the spirit. Now I came up here to get you because Amanda's got a sick horse she needs to tend. You up for standing in for her in the breeding barn? Hercules has some orders to fill." She chuckled.

Hercules was Pacific Vista Ranch's prize stallion. Horse farms around the country paid top dollar for the chance to breed their mares with his bloodline. And that took work with a phantom mare and a laboratory.

"Wherever you need me. Am I allowed to make a fluffer joke like Holt did when you first met?" Sam and Holt's first meeting was infamous. Holt had made an off-color joke in Sam's barn, Sam's legendary temper flared, and they had despised each other on sight. And then they fell madly in love and got married. He'd never seen his stepsister happier.

She elbowed him in the ribs. "One and done on that. Sorry. Come on."

He fell into step with her. "I'm still here to work for the foreseeable future. The gig is just one day."

She smiled up at him. "Soon it will be your main job again and that's fine. No offense, but part-time ranch hands are on a waiting list to work with the legendary Samantha McNeill Ericsson."

He snickered. "Legendary in your own mind. And you're making me feel cheap."

She snorted and rolled her eyes. "If the shoe fits. And you've got a spot here as long as you need it. But if you need to go, go. Just give me a week or so to replace you."

Fresh energy fueled his steps as they strode to the barn. At least it appeared his career was moving in the right direction. He'd figure out how to freelance on his terms with half the travel and at least the same amount of satisfaction.

If only he could have the same clarity for the next steps in his relationship with Livvie.

OLIVIA HIT SEND ON her email and wiggled her butt in her office chair. She'd just sent off the voluminous paperwork required for her new position in Crete. Crossed all the t's and dotted all the i's. Mrs. Sofios's assistant had confirmed that Olivia would have her very own three-bedroom place on the property, complete with panoramic sea views. She'd be restoring several different collections that the widow had acquired.

The salary was ridiculous––like jaw-dropping––especially for a librarian. To be paid to do her job, live in a Greek villa on a multi-millionaire's expansive property, and have it all sanctioned and approved by her boss here at UCSD? She laughed out loud at her good fortune.

She slid her glasses off her nose, stood, and paced around her tiny excuse for an office. Anticipation bubbled up in her chest, but it battled with the niggling vision of Grant, who hadn't been far from her heart all week. She hadn't seen him since he'd played her knight in shining armor on Saturday night. All week, she'd tossed and turned, unable to settle.

Space wasn't changing her feelings. If anything, time

apart only intensified her desire to spend as much time with him as possible.

Damn it. She wanted to be with him.

Life was short. She'd learned that lesson when her mom's life altered forever after her accident. Her own life had progressed down a different path than she'd anticipated as well. But, here she was, in a fortuitous spot. She was finally embarking on her first true adventure abroad.

Life was short. She loved Grant. She wanted to be with him, even if it was just until she left for Europe. What did she have to lose? Being apart from him while he was here was killing her. They could keep it a secret—he could come to her place, so nobody at the ranch would question her presence. They were used to seeing her Mustang over the years, but not so much overnight. Toby was spending every waking moment with Erin, so that created a buffer and its own type of shift in the Three Musketeers dynamic.

Tonight. She wasn't going to wait another minute. Her instincts urged her to text him now. Invite him over for dinner. Seduce him if need be. She had no idea what would happen when she left for Greece, but up until then she'd spend it with Grant if he was willing.

She had to try. They had a full year while she was gone to recover, so why not make it worth it? She pulled her phone out of her khaki green messenger bag and called him before she chickened out.

He answered on the second ring. "Hey, Livvie." He sounded cheerful, buoyant even.

"Hi. I'm heading out of work and have a craving for my world-famous baked salmon." Well, world-famous because it was one of a four meals she could actually prepare well. Cooking had never been her forte or her passion. "Come over for dinner—I've got news to share about Greece."

The line was silent for a few beats. "Sounds good. I'll

bring dessert--my mom dropped off some of those double fudge brownies you love so much. And I've got some news too."

Her heart gave a tug in her chest. "Oh I haven't had those in forever. Why don't you come by around six?"

"See you then."

Olivia dropped her phone back into her bag and hugged herself. New Year's Eve had been a major turning point. Finally, she was going to live an exciting life. If she had her way, she'd share every spare moment with Grant over the next six weeks, in and out of bed. She was determined to squeeze every ounce of joy and happiness. As long as he said yes.

Grant rapped on the cherry red front door of Olivia's Solana Beach Spanish-style cottage. She'd totally scored with the place, which was on a quaint residential street, a few blocks from the Cedros Shopping District, home of the world-famous Belly Up Tavern concert venue. They'd been attending live shows there from the time Livvie got her driver's license.

A colleague of hers had known the landlord, who only rented to referrals. The fact that Livvie was an archivist librarian who worked at the Geisel Library at UC San Diego had made her a shoo-in. She put the "R" in responsible.

Olivia flung open the door and stepped in for a hug before he had a chance to react. She slid her slender arms around his waist and pressed her body against his. Her soft breasts smashed against him and her fresh peach-honey scent surrounded him. He hardened. Everywhere.

He retreated a step. *Friends.* To regain their friend-zone footing, maintaining some physical space from her was vital. The feel of her and the scent of her were too much. He held up the foil-covered plate of brownies. "Don't crush the dessert." Unoriginal, but the best he could muster on the fly.

She rolled her eyes, grinned, and headed inside. "Don't worry. Come on back to the kitchen and bring the baked goods."

"Aren't you going to give me the grand tour?" He kept his gaze over her shoulder so he wouldn't be tempted to fixate on the sweet sway of her hips as she walked inside.

A small crease formed between her brows. "I can't believe you haven't been here before. Still. It's tiny, but it's perfect."

Kind of like you. He pushed away the thoughts of her perfection and shifted his focus to checking out the cottage. The old-school plaster walls were a creamy white, the front and side wall windows were square and large, the floors an antiqued walnut hardwood. Although it was rented as a studio cottage, an alcove opened off to the right that served as Livvie's den, with floor to ceiling bookshelves overflowing with an eclectic mix of paperbacks and hardcovers, organized by color.

"It's great and the high ceilings definitely make it feel bigger." He followed her into an unusually large kitchen, their footsteps catching squeaks in the floor. "And it's creaky."

"Right? It was built in the 1940s. So the kitchen is the biggest room and the bedroom is basically a closet. Check out the stove, how cool is that?" She gestured toward an enormous old-fashioned gas stove that was gleaming white and aqua with chrome accents.

"And it works?" It looked like an antique, not a functioning appliance.

She nodded. "The salmon and vegetables are just about ready. And look at the tile. The whole place is like stepping back in time."

He glanced at the Parisian-style black and white tile floor, the picture window over the farmer's sink, and agreed. He sniffed the air, the scent of lemon and rosemary making his mouth water. "Can't wait for your lemon pepper salmon. I brought a French Chablis you'll love. I discovered it when I was in France and they carry it at grocery stores here. Go figure."

"Will you open the wine? Glasses are on the shelf next to the sink. I was just about to take everything out and plate it." She turned and bent forward to open the oven door.

His gaze snagged on the way her soft faded jeans stretched across the gentle curve of her ass. Then he pivoted away toward the sink before he gripped her hips and the night spun out of control. He'd underestimated the power of her presence.

Tonight she'd worn her hair in a high ponytail, and from what he could tell, she wasn't wearing makeup. He raised his eyes up in thanks that she'd not worn that damn poppy red lipstick, which sent his mind spiraling into all kinds of places it shouldn't go. But her unpainted pale pink lips were just as tempting.

He grabbed the old-school corkscrew off the counter and opened the wine. Focused on pouring it into the stemless glasses and filing the inappropriate thoughts deep into the vault. Focused on acting like Livvie's best friend. When he turned back, she was arranging salmon filets, with small roasted red potatoes and asparagus on two large plates.

"Simple but yummy. I'll take the plates if you bring the wine and we'll eat in the living room." Her eyes crinkled at the corners and she swept her arm, emphasizing the lack of any type of dining table. "You know, skip the formal dining room."

His lips twitched. "Dining rooms are overrated."

They sank down into a plum-colored velvet sofa, but Grant was careful to maintain some distance between them.

He sipped the crisp, cold drink and surveyed the room. Precisely stacked piles of books sat on the edge of the coffee table and end tables.

A modestly sized flatscreen was mounted over a white-washed brick fireplace, framed blown-up photographs of scenes around the globe adorned the pale walls. Something shifted in his chest. They were photos he'd sent her over the years.

"You hung my photos." He stared at her, oddly flattered. Humbled.

Her lips curved up. "Of course I did. Sometimes when I was feeling particularly stuck, just seeing the pictures of all these places helped get me through. You'd always show me where you were staying on our video calls, but the photos really made it feel more real somehow. And knowing you'd taken the time to grab scenic shots for me made me really happy. You're incredible."

A flush heated the back of his neck. "You're biased. But I am pretty damn good. It went both ways––taking the time to get you pictures I knew you'd love forced me off the adrenaline high of all sports, all the time. Helped me appreciate how fortunate I've been with my career."

She picked up her plate, tucked her slender legs beneath her, and considered him. "I'm glad. Don't let the salmon get cold or it will be disgusting. And tell me your news first because I plan on going on and on and on about Crete." She popped a crisp potato into her mouth.

"Well, you know I made a bunch of calls letting people know that I was shifting from working the pro tours to freelance gigs. And I got one this weekend up in Huntington Beach." He paused and sampled the fish, which was tangy and delicious. "Dinner is awesome."

"Thanks. And that's wonderful. You've made a lot of industry contacts over the years, right?" She lifted her glass.

"Yeah, and they've been great about referring me. They know my work and are willing to pay." He tapped her wineglass before drinking. "At least enough of them will pay well to make it worth my while."

The tiny crease between her brows deepened. "Even with traveling half as much? Not to be nosy, but does freelancing pay that well?"

"It should. And I invested a lot of what I made over the last decade. So I can afford to try a different lifestyle. Maybe more local scenery shoots or something. But talking about money is boring. Tell me about Crete--you're working for some eccentric old lady?"

She laughed. "That's one way to describe her, but I think she'd prefer something more like trailblazing literature collector. You aren't going to believe this. After I basically shared every detail of my life for all the security clearances and such, her assistant Niki sent over photos of the villa that will be mine. An entire villa! Right on the water. It's like a dream." Her enthusiasm was infectious.

"Now that's first-class travel. Hell, I slept on the floor or camped in several of the locations we'd go on. And what exactly will you be doing? Organizing books or documents?"

Livvie set down her plate and shifted more fully to face him, her slim hands clasped in her lap. "Some of both. After her husband died, Mrs. Sofios came into a major fortune. She's always loved ancient literature, poems, stories and the like. She acquired some private collections at auction and I'll be cataloguing it all, reviewing it, restoring it as needed, although that's not my expertise. I've even got authority to hire an assistant."

"It does sound like someone waved a magic wand and came up with a position just for you--a villa on Crete, with a view of the sea, all the ancient texts you could want, and lots of cash? I'd say you hit the lottery. And it's so well-deserved." Warmth flooded through his system--simple joy to see his beloved friend finally getting the break she deserved.

Her gaze locked with his, joy shining in her eyes that were as blue as the sea she'd soon be waking to every morning. She licked her lips and suddenly he was fixated on her full mouth, a visceral memory of those lips wrapped around him surging through his system.

"Grant." Her pupils dilated and she started to scoot toward him. Panic flared. If he touched her right now, this tentative return to being simply best friends would implode.

He shot to his feet. "Where's the bathroom?" Although her place was the size of a postage stamp, he could clearly see it through the open archway by the fireplace.

She lowered her thick dark lashes and picked up her wine. "Right in front of you." The effervescence in her voice fizzled.

"Right. Be right back." He fled into the tiny bathroom. Like a chickenshit. Damn it, maybe having dinner alone at her house hadn't been smart. Obviously, he couldn't control his impulses and her long glances were more flirtatious than friendly.

He gripped the porcelain sink, stared at himself in the mirror, and blew out a jagged exhale. He'd known they'd have an awkward stage after Mammoth, but damn. They needed more time--probably her full year abroad--in order to find a new dynamic. The old one was gone forever--it would never be the same. But they could create a new relationship where they were friends and the sex was a distant memory.

Sex. Damn, he wanted to rush back to the couch, strip off the layers of her clothes until every single inch of her tight little body was bare to him. Take his time kissing her from head to toe. He flipped on the cold faucet and splashed his face with water. It would have to do until he could get home and take matters into his own hands. Or hand, like he'd been doing all week with the various visions of Livvie playing on repeat in his mind.

He opened the door and glanced to his right, where a queen-sized bed filled a room the size of a closet. He hurried past; nope, not looking at where Livvie laid her beautiful head every night.

The living room was empty and he found Livvie stacking their dishes to soak in bubbly water. "One downside to the vintage charm is no dishwasher." She kept her gaze focused on the sink.

Determined to salvage the night if it killed him, Grant strode to the small butcher block island where he'd set down the plate of brownies. They'd share dessert, finish the wine, and he'd escape without causing any more trouble.

Every time he was with her and didn't touch her was another battle won. Episode by episode, they'd find their footing again. Hopefully before she left for a year. They had to salvage their relationship—he couldn't survive without her. He'd missed talking to her this week.

"Better you than me." He unwrapped the foil covering the brownies. "Brownie time. Angela frosted these ones and added M&Ms too."

She gave a breathy moan. "Frosting and M&Ms? If I must."

His dick twitched. She really needed to stop with the noises. He might not survive the rest of the evening. So much for self-control.

He carried the brownies out—no need to dirty another dish—and set them on the low wood and stone coffee table. He jolted when Livvie bumped him with an elbow and handed him his wine.

"You're jumpy tonight. Relax. It's just me." She examined

the plate and selected the largest brownie, a corner piece with a mountain of frosting.

His shoulders relaxed--it was familiar sweet-toothed Olivia again. "I knew you'd pick that one." He grabbed the brownie closest to him. He'd already had two this afternoon, but Livvie didn't need to know that.

She grinned and peeked at him through her lashes. "You calling me predictable, Michaels?" Then she chomped an enormous bite and chewed, the pleasure on her face obvious.

"I wish." If only they could go back to before New Year's Eve. Something tightened in his chest--but then he wouldn't have experienced what love was supposed to feel like. The timing sucked. He took another bite and savored the sugar bomb exploding on his tongue.

"That's me. Boring, predictable librarian Olivia. But not for much longer. Soon I'll be that wild American woman ex-pat, floating in the Aegean sea."

He snorted. "You are not boring." His gaze locked on a huge smear of chocolate frosting at the corner of her mouth. "But you have chocolate all over your face."

Without thinking, he leaned in and brushed his thumb along her soft skin. Her breath caught and before he could move, she turned her head and ran her tongue around his thumb. The air thickened and her blue eyes stared into his. When he didn't pull away, couldn't pull away, she closed her lips around him and sucked.

"Fuck it." He definitely wasn't a saint. He muttered under his breath and they dove for each other. He picked her up and placed her over his lap. She rocked against him and moaned low in her throat when her center connected with his erection.

He caught her ponytail, held her head in place, and captured her mouth, her tempting, teasing mouth. Their tongues stroked and swirled, her breath a sweet combination of sugar and Livvie. She slanted her mouth across his, deepening the kiss, her taut nipples burning into him through their clothes.

He released her on a growl and grabbed the hem of her sweater and whipped it off over her head, tossing it across the room. Her breasts were displayed in a lacy pink bra and she arched her back. He slid his hands up her slender torso and lightly pinched her nipples, the way he remembered drove her wild.

"Livvie." He lowered his head and caught one breast in his mouth, tonguing her rosy peak through the soft fabric. The faint scent of peaches, honey, and clean skin was one hundred percent Olivia.

She dug her fingers into his hair. "Please. I want you."

He blew out a breath and sat back, struggling for control. "Damn it, I can't keep my hands off you. I'm trying to be good."

She spoke fast, her breath coming in short pants. "Oh, you're good. I want your hands on me. I was going to proposition you tonight. See if we could be together until I leave. Please. Life is short and I've never felt like this."

His hands tightened around her waist, his blood roaring through his veins. "But--"

She pressed one slim finger against his mouth and stared down at him, her pupils dilated, her cheeks flushed. "It can be our secret. And nothing will ever change how much we love each other."

Something tugged in his chest at the word love. When her fingers wove into his hair and she lowered her mouth to his, reason disappeared and sensation triumphed. He slid his hands up her bare back, tugged her closer, and deepened the kiss.

Her busy hands gripped the hem of his t-shirt. "This. Off." She murmured against his mouth.

Happy to oblige, he shifted and raised his arms overhead. The shirt was half-on, half-off when someone banged on the front door. Livvie yelped and scooted off his lap.

He frowned and pulled the material back down over his torso. "You expecting someone?"

"Livvie, you home?" Toby's voice said from the front porch.

"Oh no." She hissed and pulled her top over her head and smoothed down her bangs. "Give me a second, Toby," she called toward the door.

"Oh shit." Grant leapt to his feet, his mouth dry, his stomach coiling into knots. "Just act normal--we're just having dinner. No big deal."

Olivia's face had gone sheet white and she stood still as a statue. Their gazes locked, but neither of them budged.

"You gonna let me in or what?"

Grant blew out a breath, turned the doorknob, and hoped for the best. "Hey, Toby."

CHAPTER 22

Olivia cleared her throat, and tried to ignore the trembling in her legs. "Come on in."

"Hey, you guys hanging out without me?" Toby joked.

She shook her head. "Don't be silly. We were just talking earlier and decided to have dinner last-minute."

"Yeah," Grant said.

Toby studied both of them for a minute. "Something's up with you two. I could feel it on the ride back from Mammoth. Spill it."

"What do you mean?" Grant asked.

At the exact time she said, "What do you mean?"

Toby raked his hand through his russet hair. "It just feels weird. Are you guys pissed about me spending so much time with Erin? I haven't exactly been the best about seeing you both. I'm sorry."

Olivia swallowed hard, guilt a knot in her belly. "Of course that's not it. We're happy seeing you so happy with her. Right?"

Grant nodded.

"You know you can tell me. You know how much I hate

secrets. So if you're mad, tell me. We'll figure it out." Toby swung his gaze between them.

Olivia winced at Toby's erroneous assumption. No way could they allow him to think he'd done anything wrong. But without Grant's agreement, she wasn't going to share the truth. Not tonight anyway.

"Dude, you're overreacting. Everything's cool." Grant's voice was subdued.

Toby blew out a breath. "Sorry to freak out. I'd texted you a few times because you left some file in the car. I'm meeting Erin at the Belly Up to see that Pink Floyd cover band and figured I'd drop it off." He pulled a rolled document out of the back pocket of his faded jeans and handed it to her.

"Thanks." Her fingers curled around the papers. One hand pressed into her jittery, roiling belly. Toby feeling guilty that dating Erin was harming their friendship was too much. Not when she and Grant were keeping a major secret from him. Toby was easygoing about everything except for honesty. Liars were his kryptonite. They had to fix this.

The guys needed to go. *Now.* She had about T minus two minutes before she broke down and she didn't want either of them to witness it. She needed to be alone to process it all.

Grant spoke before she could ask them to leave. "I have an early morning tomorrow, so I'll walk out with you. Thanks for dinner, Livvie." He gave a half-wave and strolled out the door.

Toby's eyes softened and searched her face. "I've got to meet Erin. Promise you tell me if something's up, okay? And let's all get together next weekend, deal?"

Olivia blinked fast, not allowing the moisture in her eyes to spill over. "Of course."

He pulled her into a fierce hug. "I love you and I'm going to miss you, girl."

She squeezed him tight. "I love you too." She stepped back and managed a wobbly smile. "Now go have fun with Erin."

After he left, she turned the deadbolt with a decisive click. A weight settled on her heart and she stumbled over to the couch and pitched herself head first onto it. Grabbed the ruby colored faux-fur throw pillow and buried her face into the soft fabric. She rolled to one side, curling her knees up into a fetal position, and willed her body to stop quaking.

Every inch of her vibrated from her scalp to her toenails and a deep sob welled up in her throat. The tears came, pouring down her face in hot streams. She cried until she felt hollowed out. She rolled onto her back, keeping the pillow hugged in tight, and stared up at the smooth ceiling.

Could they have had a closer call with Toby? What if he'd knocked on the door ten minutes later? Keeping secrets was wrong. Keeping secrets from your closest friends was worse than wrong. The entire situation had emphasized how vital it was to be honest in relationships.

Which in turn hammered home the point that she hadn't been truthful with Grant. Not really. Sure, she'd admitted she'd hoped that dinner would lead to them ending up in bed tonight. But she hadn't planned on revealing the actual truth--she was in love with him.

Toby's interruption had been a bucket of freezing water. Things weren't the same. And sure, maybe after a year abroad they could be if he didn't return her feelings.

The truth was she wanted Grant for more than her best friend.

She wanted Grant for her partner, her lover, her person. Nothing would change for her while she was in Crete. In the depths of her heart, down to the marrow of her bones, she was in love with Grant. Nobody else would do for her.

So where did that leave her? Did she tuck away her feelings until she left and allow them to get back on even ground? Let Grant heal from his divorce and figure out his new day-to-day? Because she wanted to spend as much time as possible with her best friends before she left the country. And she wasn't sure she could move forward until she cleared the air.

She sat up, placed her feet on the solid hardwood floor, and set the pillow against the edge of the sofa. Nothing was happening tonight. Not with Grant as spooked as he'd been when he bailed. He'd be brooding for at least tonight and more likely the next few days. One benefit of knowing him so well, was she knew when he was upset, he needed time alone. To allow things to percolate.

Tonight she'd allow herself time to reflect. Cleaning helped her process her emotions, sort through her thoughts. She stood and snatched up one of the brownies. It would be silly to allow them to go to waste. She bit in and savored the explosion of chocolate decadence on her tongue and headed into the kitchen. She'd clear up the dinner dishes and then scrub the room, beginning with the counters all the way down to the baseboards.

In a few hours, she'd have a plan. She'd figure out how to tell Grant how she really felt and let the cards fall. Friends were always honest with each other and they couldn't have secrets now. Her heart tightened in her chest--*please don't let my declaration of love end my most meaningful relationship.*

GRANT SMACKED his palm against the steering wheel for the twentieth time. He should be smacking his head against the solid surface, but that wouldn't get him back to the ranch. He'd cursed and muttered the entire drive. Tonight had been too close of a call. If Toby had walked in on him and Livvie naked on the couch, it would have been a disaster.

He navigated through the West Gate onto the ranch, waving at Bo, the new guard. He'd gotten used to having locked and secured entrances to the ranch ever since the paparazzi had resurrected the McNeill family drama a few years ago. Making sure his family was protected, especially on their own property, was important.

Just like he should have protected Livvie instead of standing there like a dolt while Toby questioned them. Hell, protected Toby from ever feeling like he'd done something wrong.

He parked in front of the guesthouse and turned off the ignition. But he couldn't seem to reach for the door handle. He rested his arms on the steering wheel and dropped his head onto his forearms. Acknowledged the pit in his belly and the rapid pace of his breathing. Adrenaline--the itch between his shoulder blades to go to the next place. To say fuck it and just take off.

Because he felt closer to Olivia than any woman he'd been involved with romantically. An image of her supple, toned legs wrapped around him, her full pink lips plump from his kisses, and her silky skin glowing with passion flashed through his system. Her scent, an intoxicating combination of peach and honey and Olivia, drove him wild. He stiffened, his body betraying him.

But Livvie was leaving. He needed to let her go. He worked to slow down his inhales and exhales, counting to four each cycle.

A tap on the window had him yelping and jumping in his seat. His mom was standing next to his vehicle, a crease between her dark eyebrows, her hands on her hips. He shook off the reaction, tugged on the door handle, and got out of the car.

"Mom, you almost gave me a heart attack. What are you doing sneaking around in the dark?" Offense was the best defense and no way could he hide his feelings from her. Better to avert her at the pass.

One corner of her mouth twitched, but the concern coloring her eyes remained. "I wanted to talk to you about Ryan returning home soon, so I figured I'd come chat with you in person. And then I find you hunched over your steering wheel. What's up, honey?"

"Just tired. Can we talk tomorrow instead? I'm beat." No way was he up for a discussion with his mom tonight.

She cheerfully ignored him and threaded one arm through his. "Let's go inside. Just for a few minutes."

Shit. "Okay. Did Ryan call or something?" Deflect to his older brother.

"Yes, he did. He's coming home early––late March. Something about a big business opportunity with a few friends and Austin that can't wait." She crossed through the foyer and sat on the charcoal gray sofa.

That caught his attention. "Wow, that's soon. And Austin is going to work with Ryan? Seriously?" Austin was the black sheep of the family, so this was news.

"I know you two haven't been as close, but he's really turned things around. I think it's wonderful. You're okay with them living here in the guesthouse, at least at first?"

He shrugged, but his mind was racing. "There's plenty of space. What happened to Austin's girlfriend? Weren't they living together in Manhattan?"

His mom frowned. "They broke up. He wouldn't talk about it. We never met her anyway." She reclined back against the sofa and crossed one leg over the other. "Please tell me what's wrong. Is it Callie?"

Grant jolted, then shook his head. He hadn't thought about Callie at all. Huh. So he was really over her. "No, we were done a few years ago. It just took a while for the paperwork to catch up."

She hmmm'd. "Is it Olivia?"

Grant snapped his head toward her, his eyes wide. "Olivia? What do you mean?"

Her lips curved up. "I think you know what I mean."

"I…" Did she really suspect or know?

"You two have always loved each other. The three of you kids have the sweetest, tightest friendship I've ever witnessed. But you and Livvie share something more. We all noticed it at the barbeque--sparks were crackling around you two." Her eyes were soft, her smile gentle and she laid one hand on his arm. "I've just been waiting for you to realize that your person has been in front of you all along."

Something constricted in Grant's throat. "Are you serious? Why didn't you ever say anything?"

She shook her head. "It's not up to me to point it out. When you married Callie, you seemed happy at first, but then you weren't. She wanted to change who you were. Olivia loves you for who you are."

He wiped his palms on his jeans and blew out a breath. "Yeah. And I just realized I love her. Like really love her. She's the one who has always been there for me, over the distance. She was who I'd talk to before I went to sleep on the road. But it's a total mess. She's leaving in March for a year and I can't ask her to stay."

"No, you can't. She needs her time to explore the world, like you have. Can you wait for her for a year?"

His gut clenched. "A year feels like forever. And I committed to myself to root myself to one place. To prove to myself that I can be grounded and create a stable home without being on the road more often than not."

"It's kind of like a flip, right? Livvie had to stay here and care for her mom while you and Toby went off to school and then off to see the world. Now you're back and she's leaving."

"The timing sucks." He dropped his head into his hands again.

She stroked one hand through his hair, like she did when he was a child. "I understand you want to prove to yourself you can settle in one spot. But do you really need to? Travel is in your blood. Photography is your passion--I think you can figure out a way to feel more grounded. Home doesn't have to be one place. Home can be a person. Like your father was and how Chris is for me now. Think about it."

He lifted his head and looked at this incredible woman. "How did I get so lucky to have you as my mom?"

She grinned. "Obviously you are blessed. But seriously honey, think about it. I would love to have you underfoot and living here, but I want you to be happy. Whatever that looks like. Have you told Olivia how you feel?"

He winced. "No. And tonight was awkward when Toby came by. He doesn't know and we need to tell him. And I need to apologize."

"Apologize and lay out your feelings on the line. To both of them. Toby can handle it. You three have been friends for twenty years, it's okay if the friendship changes. I think you and Livvie may just be able to figure out how to have it all. You deserve it."

An idea popped up in his mind. Something that might just show Livvie how he felt and give her a choice. Now he needed to figure out how to get her to see him again after the way he'd bolted out tonight.

Groveling. It would require some serious groveling.

Grant powered down his phone and leaned forward, bracing his elbows on his thighs. He'd set the wheels in motion and some of the heaviness lifted from his shoulders. His pulse pounded and when he stood, his knees weren't altogether steady.

But he was determined to lay it all on the line for Olivia. To risk his heart. To risk a rift in their friendship. To see if he could be lucky in love the second time around.

He crossed to the granite island and double-checked the contents of his backpack. The portable speaker was there. The bottle of Veuve––Livvie's favorite fancy champagne and the framed photograph. He glanced up at the enormous kitchen clock––it was go time. He zipped the bag closed and grabbed his keys. Livvie should be arriving home from work in about fifteen minutes and he planned to be there when she pulled up.

He blasted The Cure on the drive over to Solana Beach. Not "Boys Don't Cry," but another song he hoped would relay his feelings to Livvie. Music was one of their things and if he could soften her up with a song, maybe she'd consider his proposition.

When he pulled up across from her cottage, her vintage baby blue car wasn't parked in the narrow driveway. He could wait. He turned off the engine and flipped to the next song on the album, the familiar melody washing over him. His eyes closed and his fingers tapped on the steering wheel.

The final song of the playlist faded to black and still Livvie wasn't home. He checked his phone, but there wasn't a single message. Not that she was expecting him, but she was a creature of habit, which is why he'd figured he could time his appearance perfectly.

He winced and shifted in his seat. Well, he'd sit here until she came home. However long it took. Even if the champagne grew warm.

Another ten minutes passed. Would he have to rethink his brilliant plan? Damn it, he'd text her and check in. Even though they hadn't communicated since last night. Just as he was typing, the smooth roar of her engine turned onto the street and she pulled into her driveway.

His heart hammered against his ribs and his palms were damp. He squared his shoulders, grabbed his bag, and opened the door. She was still sitting in her car when he crossed the street, and paused a few feet away.

She turned and looked at him, her dark eyebrows raised, her lips parted in surprise. She opened the door and flashed a length of toned leg when she climbed out. Carefully closed and locked the door.

"Livvie." His voice cracked. He swallowed and tried again. "Livvie, I need to talk to you. Can I come in?"

She nibbled on that full, tempting lower lip and studied him. "I didn't expect to see you so soon."

"Can we go inside?"

She nodded and marched up the two stone steps to the cherry red stoop and unlocked the front door. "You coming?" She called over one slim shoulder.

He hurried and followed her inside, closing the door behind him. She dropped her bag on the small table next to the front door and crossed her arms. The move tightened the silky jade-colored fabric of her dress across her chest. She looked like every fantasy of a sexy librarian with her conservative dress, her high top-knot with a pencil stuck through it, and her Mary Jane heels.

"Do you want a beer or should we just talk?" Her eyes widened, but her expression gave nothing away.

His pulse kicked into high gear and sweat prickled on the back of his neck. "Let's talk first. Can we sit while I set a few things up?"

"Set things up?"

He unzipped the backpack, pulled out the speaker, and powered it on. "I want to play a song for you." He set it on the coffee table and sank onto the couch.

She skirted around the opposite edge of the table, perched on the far end of the sofa, and rested her clasped hands on her thighs. "I have some things to say to you too."

"And I want to listen. Okay if I go first?"

She gestured with one hand. "Sure."

He tapped his phone and hit play. The first bars of the song he'd chosen emerged through the speaker, filling the room with its uplifting beat.

Her jaw relaxed and her lips curved upward. "'Lovesong'?"

He pulled out the framed photo and set it next to the speaker. He moved closer and grasped her hands, intertwined his fingers with her slender ones. "I told you how that night in the car listening to The Cure stuck with me, right?

And I know your favorite song is 'Boys Don't Cry,' but this is mine. It makes me think of you and smile. Just like the snow angels remind me of how much fun we have together."

She gazed over at the photo of her in the snow and her smile grew cheeky. "Yeah? I love that picture. It was fun, but I wish I had one of right after I caught you with the epic snowball."

"Yeah. I'm not good at this, so I'm just going to put it all out there." He drew a fortifying breath. "Toby reminded me that without honesty, relationships can't really exist. So I'm going to be honest. I love you, Olivia Hanlon. I love you as my best friend. As the person who always held my heart close and who always got me, even when most people don't. You see me––who I really am beneath what most people see. And you accept me for me."

"I do love you just how you are. But I––"

"Please let me finish––I need to say the important part. I see you too, Livvie. You're the most compassionate, generous, loyal, funny, sweet and brilliant person I know. You're one of the best people I know. I admire your drive and determination and how despite having so much responsibility a such a young age, you still pushed through and realized your dreams." He paused for a moment to catch his breath. "I love you."

Olivia leapt into his lap, wrapped her arms around his neck, and pressed her soft lips against his. "I love you too."

His arms banded around her and cautious joy warmed his chest. "You do?"

She tilted her head back, her azure gaze locked with his. "Yes, I do. I was figuring out how to tell you and you beat me to it."

He captured her mouth, her lips parting against his, their tongues dancing leisurely together. Her delicious scent enveloped him and the heat of her body settled against him.

She shifted back and his arms tightened--unwilling to let her go. "I think I've always loved you. I didn't realize it, but subconsciously I think I compared every guy I dated to you. And when they didn't measure up--and nobody did--I'd break it off. I love your strength, and your active seeking mind, your ability to capture and create magic through your photos. Your loyalty to your family and to me. The way you've always listened to me, always been the voice in the dark soothing me to sleep, no matter how many miles separated us."

Warmth surged through him. "Your voice did the same for me, no matter where I was." She'd been his compass. His sense of home.

"I'm not finished. And I love your hard, sexy body. That's what sealed the deal for me." She wiggled her hips.

He threw back his head and laughed. "I knew it. You just wanted me for the sex."

She nodded and smoothed her hands over his chest. "Well, playing The Cure for me was a smart move too. Acknowledging my superior taste in music."

"And we need to tell Toby. Assure him that nothing will change our friendship--no more secrets."

"I was going to say the same thing. I think when we explain it all, he'll be fine. The bottom line is that our friendship has changed and will change over the years. I mean, if he ends up with Erin, that's a change, right? As long as we don't hide anything, we can make it a new version of the Three Musketeers."

He smiled, dove into the rest of his plan. "Exactly. We'll tell him this week. One more thing. I think I've figured out a way to make the distance work for the next year."

Her brows drew together. "Don't remind me we only have weeks."

He held up one hand. "Or not. This is your decision, but I

made some calls and it just so happens I've got some industry contacts in France and Italy. Who were more than happy to learn I could be available for freelance work." His pulse accelerated again. "So, if I had a home base somewhere near one of those countries, I'd be able to take short projects."

Livvie drew back, her eyes wide. "What are you saying?"

"I'm saying that I realized I don't have to settle at the ranch to prove some point to myself. That I can still be flexible. So if in a few months' time, some gorgeous brunette invited me to stay with her in a fancy villa, I could do that and also work."

"What?" She squealed and hugged him. "You're saying you'll come to Greece with me?"

"I'm saying it is your choice. You have this opportunity in Crete. I'm saying if you wanted me there with you, I would love to go. But if you want to do this all on your own, I totally respect that. I'll miss the hell out of you, but we can plan some visits. Make it work. It's just a year." His belly tensed. He sure as hell didn't want to wait a year for them to truly be together as a couple, but it was up to Olivia.

"Yes, yes, yes! I want you there and Niki told me I could bring family or whoever to the villa. I'm sure I could ask and they'd be fine with it. I would love for you to come with me. And I'll still be doing the job on my own, even if you're who I'm with off-hours."

Joy pumped through him, hot and fast. "Are you sure? Because I'm ready to go anytime. We could wait until you're settled in before I join you."

She nodded, her eyes gleaming. "We'll figure it out. Having you with me will only make the experience sweeter. You've made me the happiest woman in the world."

"Same. I brought a bottle of Veuve. Let's pop it and celebrate."

She clasped his cheeks between her hands and kissed him. "Bubbly and then let's get naked and dance around the house to celebrate."

He laughed. "I'll dance with you, just this once. Just close the blinds."

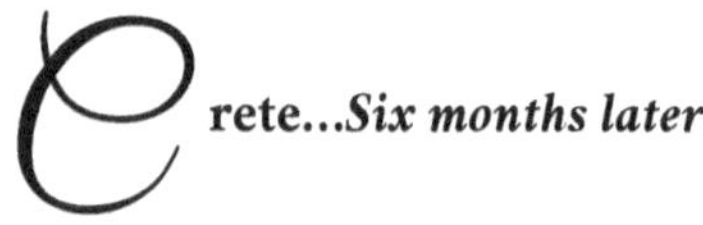

rete...*Six months later*

OLIVIA PLACED her leather-tooled notebook and fountain pen onto the stone patio table, stretched her arms overhead, and savored the kiss of salty sea breeze on her face. She'd been basking in the glorious July warmth, like one of Mrs. Sofios's four dainty cats who roamed the private estate in the Agios Nikolaos area of Northern Crete. She'd fallen madly in love with Gaia, Calypso, Ares, and Apollo, and the sweet felines enjoyed lounging in the sunshine with her.

Calypso, a tiny snow-white cat with one blue eye and one amber eye, threaded around her feet, and purred. No doubt her toe tapping and constant watch checking alerted the sensitive animal to Olivia's excitement. Time was crawling today and she was eager for the moment she could leave for the Heraklion Airport and pick up Grant, who was arriving in a few hours. Finally.

She'd settled into her new life in Greece––because living

in a breathtaking villa on the main property of Villa Freya, a luxurious sprawling hilltop estate--was such a hardship. Mrs. Sofios was lovely, the priceless collections she was curating were fascinating, and Olivia pinched herself on the daily each morning she woke in paradise. She grinned and stroked the cat's velvety soft fur and admired the sweeping views of the pristine cerulean sea and distant mountains.

But it had been four months since she'd seen Grant, except for on their nightly FaceTime calls. When they'd decided together Olivia should establish herself in her new role in Crete before Grant joined her, it had all sounded smart and sensible. The practical and the mature path to follow.

Maturity was overrated. She missed him. They'd only had weeks together after they'd discovered their love for each other before she earned the first stamp on her brand new passport.

All four cats leapt up suddenly and padded silently toward the broad open doorways of the creamy stone and glass villa. Olivia stood and donned the gauzy pale blue cover-up, in case any of the Sofios family or staff were dropping by. Not that Mrs. Sofios cared that Olivia enjoyed working by her private villa's pool, but the Greeks were more formal and running around in her scarlet polka-dot bikini wasn't done.

Footsteps echoed on the marble flooring inside and Olivia checked her watch again--she didn't have any scheduled appointments today or tomorrow. Unless in her giddiness over Grant's arrival she'd forgotten one. Definitely a possibility today. She adjusted the broad brim of her straw hat and strolled toward the house. Time to head inside anyways.

A tall, lean-framed man stood silhouetted in the entrance and Olivia blinked, her eyes adjusting from the blazing sun to the shadowy space. Maybe the light was playing tricks on her, but this guy looked like Grant. Who was not scheduled to arrive from Athens until 5:10 p.m.

She stopped and whipped off her sunglasses. Her pulse skipped in her veins--and a tingle of excitement skated down her spine.

"Livvie." He crossed the space between them and swept her up into his arms, hugging her into his solid chest.

She laughed and threw her arms around his neck, the faint scent of laundry detergent and warm male skin surrounding her. "What are you doing here?"

He angled his head back, a cheeky grin on his suntanned face. "Umm, I'm moving here, remember?"

"I mean how did you get here so early? I thought you were on the afternoon flight?" She thrust her fingers into his windswept hair and gazed into his honey-gold eyes.

He pressed his lips to hers in a quick kiss. "I wanted to surprise you so I came in a day early. It looks like you're surprised?"

"Yes. But in the best way. I can't believe you're finally here." She framed his lean cheeks between her hands. "You're finally here."

"I'm here." He slanted his mouth across hers and her lips parted, welcoming the stroke of his tongue against hers. He growled and deepened the kiss and pure joy took hold.

Several minutes later, he lifted his head. "I've missed you, Livvie." He pressed a kiss on the tip of her nose. "I don't want to be separated from you for this long again."

A wave of giddiness danced through her system. "I've missed you too. Four months is definitely unreasonable. I can't wait to share Crete with you."

She clasped his hand and led him toward the edge of the terrace, where the stone met the sloping hillside down into the shimmering sea. The near-constant island breeze carried the scents of sea and aromatic plants and trees.

"I can't believe this is where we get to live together. And I've made sure the gigs I've accepted aren't longer than two weeks." He surveyed the natural beauty of the island views, his jaw relaxed, his lips curved upward.

"I guess I can handle two weeks. Maximum." She beamed at him. "So, what do you want to do first? I can take you down into Elounda, which is a cosmopolitan little town, or over to Plaka, which is an adorable village. Toby and Erin are going to be blown away when they come in September. There's so much to see, so much history. I mean, the fireplace in Mrs. Sofios' villa is six hundred years old."

He tugged her into his arms again. "We've got plenty of time to explore Crete and I can't wait to show you some of the places in other countries I photographed for you. But right now, I'm a little tired from all the travel. Maybe you could show me our bedroom?" His voice was light, but his voice deepened.

She wound her arms around his neck, rose on her tiptoes, and murmured against his lips. "Oh, how rude of me. A nice long nap is the proper way to start this next chapter of our lives."

"I thought you'd never ask." He smiled against her mouth. "And Livvie, this next chapter is the just the beginning because I never want to let you go. I love you so much."

She savored the sincerity shining in his eyes, the heat of the sun on her shoulders, and the powerful emotion beating in her heart. "I love you, Grant Michaels. Forever."

"Forever." He swept her up in his arms and turned toward the villa. "Lead the way."

WHAT'S NEXT

Thanks so much for reading! If you have a moment, please leave a review for *The Wonder of You* on your favorite book site.

****

Ready for Grant's big brother Ryan to find love?

He's her grumpy boss. She's his nemesis. How thin is the line between love/hate?

Entrepreneur Ryan Michaels never loses. Well, except that time, a few years ago when he lost a promotion to spoiled rich girl, Charlotte "Charlie" Ray. Now he's forced to hire his nemesis to secure funding to develop a string of luxury boutique hotels. Not only does she not fit his corporate vision, but she's too damn attractive for her own good. And his.

Working as VP of Sales and Marketing for a luxury hotel is Charlie's dream job. Too bad her boss is Ryan Michaels, the same pompous stick-in-the-mud that she remembers. If he tells her that this project is his legacy one more time, she might scream. Or maybe kissing him will get him to shut up?

Because that's the other thing. The sizzling attraction between Ryan and Charlie is impossible to ignore. But everyone knows not to mix business and pleasure. Don't they?

***Hotel King is the first book in award-winning and USA Today bestselling author Claire Marti's new spin off contemporary romance series, California Suits. The series follows the adventures of five best friends who are opening a string of luxury boutique hotels from La Jolla to Monterey to Beverly Hills as each one finds true love…usually where he least expects it. Each book is a standalone.

ALSO BY CLAIRE MARTI

Pacific Vista Ranch Series

Nobody Else But You

The Very Thought of You

For The Love of You

Wrapped Up with You

The Wonder of You

You Give Good Game (related novella)

California Suits Series

Hotel King

Wine Country King

Monterey King

Holiday Queen

Palm Springs King

Beverly Hills King

True Stars Collide (related novella)

Romance in Laguna Beach Series

Second Chance in Laguna

At Last in Laguna

Sunset in Laguna

ACKNOWLEDGMENTS

Writing this book was a challenge on many levels. I lost my papa while finishing this story and let's just say I was extra emotional. Without all the love and support, I couldn't have completed it.

Big thanks for all the assistance I received from so many fabulous people. Thank you to my dear friend Dylan Jones for sharing your librarian training with me. Anna Bradley, your archivist and collection talents helped me shape Olivia. Thanks to my former yoga student Brenda Gutzie for your insight into all the ways a librarian could travel to Greece. I've got to admit, I'd love to be a librarian. Maybe if this writing gig doesn't work out…

Todd LeVeck and Chris Lowery: thanks for sharing your vast experience with photography and extreme sports production. Julie Brosseau Crocker-thanks for reminding me about all the good times we had in your 1966 Mustang––I modeled Olivia's after yours. Heidi and Jason Shurtz, thanks for insight on snowboarding and Mammoth Mountain. I want to thank my wonderful beta readers: Kay Bennett, Joanna Kelly, Sara Martin, and Serena Bell—you each help me more than you could imagine. I appreciate your time and opinions. For the lovely author friends I've made along the way, with whom I share such a sense of camaraderie, thanks for being there: Kerrigan Byrne, Anna Bradley, Krista Sandor, Liana de la Rosa, Katie O'Sullivan, Donna Simonetta, Charlotte O'Shay, Katie Baldwin, and many more.

To my wonderful editor, Lindsey Faber, thank you for

your keen insight, heavy lifting, and your brilliant ideas in making sure Grant and Olivia's story is ready for the world. Thank you Reina of Rickrack Books for your eagle eye proofreading. Thank you Christina Hovland for the beautiful covers you create.

Last but not least, to Todd for being my very own hero. I love you. And, finally to my furry kids: Lola, Beau and Josie, thanks for providing me daily laughs and all the cuddles.

ABOUT THE AUTHOR

Claire Marti is an award winning and *USA Today* Bestselling author of swoonworthy Contemporary Romance novels set in Southern California, including the California Suits series, Pacific Vista Ranch series, and the Romance in Laguna Beach series. She lives in San Diego with her husband, silly dog, and three clever cats.

Claire started writing stories as soon as she was old enough to pick up pencil and paper. After graduating from the University of Virginia with a BA in English Literature, Claire was sidetracked by other careers, including practicing law, selling software for legal publishers, and managing a non-profit animal rescue for a Hollywood actress.

Finally, Claire followed her heart and now focuses on two of her true passions: writing romance and teaching yoga.

9 781733 304696